Vivian's Window

JASON DENNIS

iUniverse, Inc.
Bloomington

Vivian's Window

This is a work of fiction. All of the characters, names, incidents,
organizations, and dialogue in this novel are either the products
of the author's imagination or are used fictitiously.

iUniverse books may be ordered through booksellers or by contacting:

iUniverse
1663 Liberty Drive
Bloomington, IN 47403
www.iuniverse.com
1-800-Authors (1-800-288-4677)

ISBN: 978-1-4759-5649-8 (sc)
ISBN: 978-1-4759-5648-1 (hc)
ISBN: 978-1-4759-5647-4 (e)

Library of Congress Control Number: 2012919524

Printed in the United States of America

iUniverse rev. date: 11/29/2012

From "Carwyn" to "endure," despite the words, time, miles, and space in between, for Valerie—who, in some way or another, was there all along.

Part 0

(RIGHT ABOUT NOW)

6

CARWYN WAS GETTING TO the point where he never exactly knew just what he might do next. Things seemed to have been going from bad to worse to just plain shitty for some months now. Perhaps, though, the worst aspect of his current state of existence was his realization that he had it a lot better than a lot of people. He had a good education. He wasn't homeless. He was a good-looking guy. He had a job. He had *potential*.

But it seemed that things were slowly starting to crack and deteriorate around him. He vacillated between thinking that his life sucked and thinking that he was a spoiled and complacent little shit. Carwyn's vacillation certainly did not help ease his frustration or his cheerlessness. Of late, he was almost always feeling frustrated about one thing or another.

He seemed to be floundering yet at the same time always on the brink of doing something. Whether that something was good, bad, indifferent, insane, dangerous, life altering, or cosmically irrelevant was another thing altogether.

Sometimes he felt like he wanted to start a fight. Sometimes he felt like he wanted to do something of great global importance. Sometimes he wanted to get in his car and drive somewhere far away and new, to hit the reset button on his adult life.

Sometimes, when he was driving, he had the strangest urge to close his eyes. He wasn't suicidal. He just wanted excitement, needed it. He just needed something, anything, to happen.

It seemed to Carwyn that things had been so much better when he had carried his lunch in a Transformers lunch box and when, according to G. I. Joe, knowing was half the battle. These days he often wished he knew half as much.

As he brushed his teeth, Carwyn examined himself in the mirror. He found himself wishing that his teeth were whiter (but not too white). He wished his

3

teeth were a little more perfectly straight. He wished he had better vision. He wished he could bench more than just 175 pounds. He wished his abs were more defined. He wasn't even out of shape. He was an athletic guy.

Well, he was athletic *looking* at least. Carwyn hadn't participated in any truly competitive athletic activities in quite some time. It had been months since his ACL surgery, and he still didn't feel comfortable doing anything even remotely athletic on it.

He wished his knee was fixed. He wished that he was fixed, that he could play in a softball league, a dodgeball league, a kickball league—anything. Carwyn's physical health and his ability to participate in athletics were such a large part of his life that he honestly felt like a part of him had died when he tore the seemingly insignificant sinew.

And then there was the damn girl. Her very name was literally sigh inducing—sometimes happy sighs, sometimes sad. He wished she would call. She would make things more ... well ... more not-so-sucky. But maybe that was wishful thinking. Maybe it had been just a stupid fling. Maybe he was romanticizing and idealizing the whole thing. Maybe he missed the idea more than the person. Yet he knew that was not the case. *Knew* it.

He wished he had more friends. Carwyn had recently moved, and he knew practically no one. He wished he was more outgoing. He wished he didn't feel like such a whining loser for wishing so many trivial things. Hell, he wished the phone would just ring, and bam, his life would change forever for the better.

Carwyn found it remarkable how much thinking one could do while simply brushing one's teeth. Sometimes mirrors (even dirty bathroom mirrors) have a funny way of making us reflect inward.

He spit out his toothpaste then gargled with some mouthwash. He actually took a pinch of pleasure from the mild alcohol burn of the green liquid as he sloshed and swished it around in his mouth. Spit. Deodorant. Rogaine. He wished he wasn't so self-conscious about his thinning hair. It wasn't even that noticeable. Only a girl taller than Carwyn might be able to notice it. And most girls, even in heels, were not taller. He wished he had less body hair. He wasn't really all that hairy. He didn't have a hairy back—just a hairy chest. Hell, some women loved a man with a hairy chest. But these days it seemed smooth was in.

"Damn," he said out loud to himself, "I really should shave today." But he just couldn't bring himself to do it. `More constant motivation. That was a big one. He wished he had a more consistent level of motivation.` Maybe then he would get more done.

He worked for Peak Performance. It was a huge outdoor sports supply store that doubled as an indoor rock-climbing gym. He didn't hate his job, but he didn't really like it either.

Carwyn hadn't been climbing in way too long—since well before his surgery—and watching all the climbers, young and old, made him a little bitter. He had been relatively new to climbing when he tore up his knee playing in an adult rec soccer league.

He had just completed a lead climbing course, had been climbing 5.10s with ease, and even started to nail some 5.11s and 12s. Carwyn's upper body strength and flexibility allowed him to compensate for his lack of proper climbing technique, but he was sure that with practice he could develop his technique and become as good a rock climber as any nonprofessional.

Carwyn had a masters in journalism, but, as he had thrown away his first (and likely only) meaningful opportunity, he had never really put his graduate education to use. He should have gone to business school or law school, somewhere he could have overspent on an education that would really have allowed him to put words to use. *The pen is mightier than the sword and all that,* he thought. *Yeah, horseshit, if you stabbed someone with the fucking pen.*

He hadn't given up all hope yet. He hadn't been thoroughly sucked into his own self-indulgent cynicism. He believed in … something. *But what?* The fledgling but potentially pure and true love that he thought he had found had apparently flitted away.

Carwyn skipped shaving, put on his company polo, and got "pumped up" about another day of selling canoes, hiking boots, and carabiners.

Part 1

(SOME MONTHS BEFORE NOW)

$$—\,1\,—$$

IT HADN'T ALWAYS BEEN this way. Carwyn hadn't always been angry at life. He used to be a lot more carefree, outgoing, and personable; and he used to take more joy from even the simplest things in life. When he got his journalism degree, he had been prepared to take the news business by storm. Despite traditional news media struggling to compete with the internet for the attention and dollars of generation Twitter, he was going to write award-winning news stories and uncover important truths. *Ha. Damn. How one year—hell, how six months—can throw one big fucking rusty old wrench straight into the heart of the ramshackle machine of life.* (He also wished he cursed just a little bit less.)

*   *   *   *

By the time he had gone back to school for his masters, it had been eight years since Carwyn and Bret had graduated together from Royal West High School. Now here they were, about to cross another stage together: Carwyn Hillis getting his Masters of Journalism and Public Policy and Bret Hightower getting his Masters of Architectural Design.

They had been best friends since high school, where the happenstance of their last names had made them lab partners their freshman year; but they had gone their separate ways upon graduation. Carwyn, who had always been good with words, had gone to a big SEC school and walked on to the soccer team. Bret, who preferred doodling instead of taking notes or paying attention in class, had gone up to the coast to a small private school in New England and had almost run off with the dean's wife.

They had found it hard to keep in touch during their undergraduate days but had always managed to catch up over the holidays and share the most outrageous of their stories.

The two were alike on certain fundamental levels, but yet very different when it came to some of the most random things. In spite of their random differences, and likely somewhat because of some them, their friendship had always remained strong. They knew everything about each other—well, almost everything.

After they earned their bachelors degrees, they both worked for two years. Neither hit it rich, and neither liked his job. They barely kept in touch with each other during that time, as neither one moved home; but one Christmas, over a case of beer, they both decided that they hated their jobs and wanted to go back to school.

They eventually resolved to try to go to the same school or at least go to schools in the same city. In their minds, that narrowed the search down to New York City, Chicago, Boston, and DC. They decided not to live together, because they both knew that even the best of friends can often make the worst of roommates.

2

BRET STARTED CASUALLY SLEEPING with an MBA student from Philadelphia in the spring of his and Carwyn's first year at Northeastern. Carwyn had to admit that Rebecca was exceptionally hot.

During the third month of their fling, before things were even serious, Rebecca took Bret for an extended weekend trip to Las Vegas. Bret was a better-than-average poker player. By Friday night, he was up about five grand. Bret, however, had little to no restraint, so by Saturday afternoon he was playing at the high stakes tables and enjoying free drinks with top-shelf liquor.

By early Saturday evening, he was about five grand in the hole. He kept digging and digging, thinking he could dig his way out, but he only succeeded in digging himself deeper. And deeper. Bret ended up in a twenty-grand hole with no way to pay it back before he finally called it a day.

That night, as Bret and Rebecca were getting ready for the Cirque du Soleil show Rebecca had suggested they see, some nice gentlemen paid a visit to their hotel room. Before the nice little visit, Rebecca was unaware of the debt Bret had accumulated.

Bret was a smooth talker and might have been able to talk his way out of any roughing up or lesson teaching or message sending (yes, he really could be that smooth), but he never even had to open his mouth. Rebecca very matter-of-factly offered to pay off Bret's debt first thing in the morning if the gentlemen in almost all black would kindly leave and let Bret and Rebecca finish getting ready for their show.

That was how Bret first learned of Rebecca's inheritance. Rebecca had told him about her parents a couple weeks before. To Rebecca, that in itself was a big step. When she told Bret about the money, Bret knew it must be love. Seriously.

By the fall of Bret and Carwyn's second (and final) year, Bret and

Rebecca were more than just casually dating, and by that December, it was legitimately serious. Carwyn had dated his fair share of girls, but whether it was him or the girls or both, none of his relationships had lasted very long. He had liked all the girls he had dated—or most of them, at least. He might have even loved a couple of them. Had he been *in love?* No, probably not. But matters of the heart (truly matters of subtle chemical variations in the brain) are definitely not an exact science.

In every relationship Carwyn had been in, despite heightened chemical concentrations and outwardly potent manifestations, whatever force had pulled Carwyn and a particular girl together simply did not last. The seemingly sweet serendipity of all the chance meetings during which Carwyn's life happened to intersect with the lives of the girls he had dated ceded to inevitability, and the chemicals, along with the feelings they triggered, subsided.

Whatever the state of Carwyn's relationship history, he was not at all surprised when Bret informed him that he had popped the question to Rebecca. And Carwyn was legitimately psyched when Bret asked him to be the best man.

The wedding date was set for the coming October, just about six months away. Carwyn was by no means an expert on the matter, but it seemed a bit quick to him—not that it should ever take that long to plan a wedding.

$$* \quad * \quad * \quad *$$

Rebecca's inheritance had come at a cost. She had lost both her parents in a tragic accident when she was about nine years old. The hefty inheritance was left in trust to her, and the trustee must have taken his duties very seriously and invested quite wisely, because when Rebecca had gained full access to the money at the age of eighteen, she had instantly become a multimillionaire (about a twenty-five millionaire, to be more precise).

Carwyn found it somewhat pretentious that Rebecca had decided to go back to school. Carwyn figured she was bored or else knew that she would quickly become bored if she didn't take certain steps to preempt the boredom. There were other things Carwyn didn't like about Rebecca, but he kept most of them to himself. Carwyn did, of course, make the requisite jokes about Bret being whipped and never getting to sleep with any other women, et cetera; but he never shared his real opinion of Rebecca. She wasn't really all that bad anyway. So it was set: Bret was taking the plunge.

3

In late March of the last year of Bret's single life, Carwyn and Bret decided that there was no better way to celebrate graduating (along with Bret's engagement) than to fly to Europe right after graduation. Bret had actually never traveled abroad. He'd seen a donkey show in Mexico, but he'd never been across the Atlantic. Carwyn had studied abroad one summer in Paris and had been to England twice. The trip would double as an extended bachelor party. Rebecca was planning on splitting her time between an internship and working on a thesis all summer.

Bret had already secured a well-paying job, and of course he was marrying into a shit ton of money, so he didn't have to worry about the cost of the trip. Carwyn knew that he couldn't really afford the trip, so he just decided not to think about the cost.

The plan that developed was to go for ten days. They purchased Eurail passes and agreed to pick three cities each. The tentative plan was to stay a day or two in each one. It would be a whirlwind tour of sorts, and if they had any time left toward the end of the trip, they would play it by ear like true backpackers. Bret, who was somewhat aware of Carwyn's financial situation, offered to pay for their hotel rooms over the course of the trip, but as he told Carwyn, that entitled him to the bed if, because of last-minute bookings, they ever got stuck in a room with only one.

"You sure you don't want to cuddle?" teased Carwyn. "I'll even let you call me Becca bear."

"Dude. Don't be gay."

"Okay, your loss. I am one amazing cuddler."

After a couple of days of deliberation, Carwyn decided on his three cities: Stockholm, Moscow, and Barcelona.

"Moscow? Bro, that's barely Europe, if at all."

"It's Europe enough, and it will definitely be different."

"Yeah, well, maybe you can find yourself a bride there. That's about the only chance you've got: to pay for it."

"Whatever, ass, what are your three?"

"Munich, Rome, and Amsterdam."

"Amsterdam, huh? You would pick that, pothead."

"I picked Amsterdam for you, bro. You'll have the chance to visit with a nice prostitute ... by the way, you ever notice that Sweden looks like a dangling penis?"

"What?"

"A dangling penis. If you ignore Norway, Sweden and Finland together look like a dangly penis and wrinkly ol' ball sack. I'm tellin' ya, Italy looks like a boot; everybody agrees on that. Most people agree that Michigan looks like a mitten, and Scandinavia looks like some dick and ballage ... look at a map, bro."

So they pulled up a map of Scandinavia on Carwyn's laptop, which was open, coincidentally enough, on an IKEA table that had taken way too long to assemble. Carwyn had to laugh. "Well, I'll be damned. It *does* look like a penis."

They examined the map a little bit longer and tentatively settled on flying into Stockholm, taking a cheap flight to Barcelona, and then taking a boat of some sort from Barcelona to Rome. After Rome, they would take the train to Amsterdam and Munich before venturing to Moscow. They would fly home from Moscow.

4

CARWYN HAD GRUDGINGLY AGREED to provide Rebecca with their general itinerary. *What harm could it really cause anyway?* And that way Rebecca would feel a little more comfortable with the trip. Bret told Rebecca he would call her every other day or so to keep her updated on where they were and what they had been seeing and doing.

Carwyn and Rebecca had the kind of love-hate relationship that is not atypical between a man's best friend and his fiancée. They got along fine, but in a quirky sort of way. They were, after all, competing for Bret's time—Carwyn for drinking beer, shooting pool, and watching action movies; Rebecca for going for coffee, shopping, and watching romantic comedies with Matthew McConaughey, one of the Cusaks, or even one of the Wilson siblings.

Bret and Carwyn's flight left on a Wednesday. They had a layover in New York and were scheduled to arrive in Stockholm around 5:00 p.m. local time. As the plane began its descent, a fat, pleasant woman seated next to Carwyn asked him if he was glad to be coming home.

"I sure am."

It must have been the blond hair and blue eyes. Bret had to hold back his laughter.

After they landed at Stockholm-Arlanda, they retrieved their luggage and decided on the Arlanda Express rail link over the Flygbussarna bus line. Once downtown, the first thing they noticed was that everybody was *not* tall and blond. They had about a three-quarter-mile walk to their hotel.

"I haven't seen any women that are Swedish Bikini Team material," commented Bret.

"You're an idiot."

"Fuck me. There's one."

"Whoa. You ain't kiddin' … she's gotta be, what, six feet tall?"

"At least, with 36 Cs. And damn, bro, I bet those legs could sure keep my ears warm."

"Keep your ears warm? We just landed, and you're already talking about burying your head in between some random Swede's legs. Tell me, why on earth are you getting married?"

"I'm just saying, Car. I mean damn, I can look, can't I? I don't actually plan on visiting her Smorgasbord."

As Stockholm was the one city for which they new exactly when they would be arriving, they had two beds in their hotel room. When they finally got to the room, they let their luggage flop to the ground; then they each flopped onto a bed.

When they woke, the sky was dark.

"Shit!"

"What?"

"It's getting darker outside. That must mean it's getting late. I think it stays light damn near forever in Scandinavia during the spring and summer months."

Bret checked the clock then looked out the window. "It's only ten after eight, bro. I think the sun just went behind a cloud or something. We have plenty of time to shower, grab a bite to eat, and then hit the town."

The plan was to hit up one of Stockholm's more fashionable nightclubs and then check out the Ice Bar. They were going to make it an early night so tomorrow they could do some sightseeing. Before they left the hotel room, Bret went rummaging through his suitcase.

"So, Car, idea: let me give you some of my business cards, you scratch out my number and e-mail address and put yours down, and that way you can give it to some attractive ladies and see if they call."

"You can't be serious?"

"Yeah. Why not, bro? It works."

"For douches. You actually brought business cards with you? You haven't even started your job yet."

"You never know when you might meet someone who has the potential to change your life forever."

"Oh, you mean like the type of girl a man would propose to? That kind of person?"

"Fortune favors the bold."

"So what, you're a horny, philandering fortune cookie, now?"

"No. I'm an opportunist. Are you takin' some or not?"

"Oh, for fuck's sake, give me some of the damn cards, but I'm putting my name on them too."

"That'll kind of screw up the whole effect," Bret said, but he gave Carwyn about a dozen of his business cards anyway. Carwyn scratched out Bret's name and number and wrote his in their place.

"Happy?"

"Very."

Bret and Carwyn looked up a few of Stockholm's swankier places on Bret's phone before they made their way out for the evening, but it didn't matter all the much. They couldn't get in to any of the places they tried. All the doormen seemed to have something against Bret's choice of footwear. They were turned away at East, Rose, Riche, Spy Bar, and Sturecompagniet.

"What the fuck?"

"You shouldn't have worn goddamn flip-flops!"

"But they're OluKai. They're like two-hundred-dollar flip-flops."

"Woopty shit. I don't care if you're strutting around in Jesus's damn sandals. Have you seen a single Swede in flip-flops? Hell, you wouldn't get into certain clubs back home in flip-flops."

"I haven't been starring at everybody's feet, bro. Why didn't you say something before?"

"I didn't notice before. So I guess the Ice Bar it is."

"Yeah, if they let us in."

"I bet your feet are going to be cold."

"Fuck off."

The Ice Bar was located inside a hotel, and Bret and Carwyn actually got in. The cover charge was something like twenty bucks. Bret paid before Carwyn even had a chance to object.

The bar was smaller than they expected. They figured it had to be small for practical purposes. And it *was* cold. Duh. Neither Bret nor Carwyn had thought to bring a hat or gloves with them—not that they had packed any to begin with. Luckily the bar provided patrons with ugly silver space-age-Eskimo-looking hooded cape things to wear. They didn't do much good for Bret's feet.

The bar had a decent crowd of attractive people, but everybody seemed to be separated off into smallish groups, uninterested in the other groups around them. One of the two should have figured that a bar where you could freeze your ass off wouldn't be the best place to meet new people. The bar wasn't actually all *that* cold, but the people certainly were, based on Carwyn's sample size of one.

A sexy Swedish girl walked up to the bar, and on a somewhat uncharacteristic whim, Carwyn decided to introduce himself: "Hi, my name's Carwyn. Can I buy you a drink?"

The sexy Swede didn't give Carwyn her name; in hindsight that should have been his first clue that he was headed down a dead-end street.

"Okay, yes. I will have an electric orchid. That is very nice of you."

She spoke very polished English with a sexy accent, but Carwyn decided not to comment. He simply conveyed the order to the bartender.

"145 crowns."

Carwyn knew that was a lot. He wasn't sure exactly how much, but beers were only forty-five, so he knew he had just shelled out a shit ton of money for one drink. He couldn't really refuse to pay for it now, so he handed over his credit card. He wasn't even the buy-girls-drinks-and-pick-them-up-at-bars type. In fact, he had bought a random girl a drink only once or twice before, and he had never used it as way to take a girl home.

"Tack. Thank you."

"You're welcome. So do you—"

But she was already walking off. *I'm not so sure I like this city,* Carwyn thought. After Carwyn put out the flames of his very efficient and explosive crash and burn, he and Bret decided to take a seat at the bar and sample some vodka. They had about three or four drinks apiece, paid way too much for them, and got way too mild a buzz. They ended up leaving early; they weren't completely over their jetlag and had plans for the next morning.

5

THE *GENTILUOMINI PRIVATI* IS an association of power and influence. It is composed of made men, politicos, judges, and law-enforcement officers on the take. The made men handle the wet work; well, they contract with a select few mechanics to fix problems whenever they arise. If somebody has to be disposed of, it gets handled. If somebody's untimely demise needs to look like an accident, an accident happens. If information needs to be extracted from a reluctant or recalcitrant individual, it is extracted. If a target has to be disappeared, so be it. If somebody is unfortunate enough to end up on the *gentiluomini's* bad side, they may as well never have existed.

The politicians, both state and federal, along with select judges, exert the appropriate influence (or lack thereof) when needed to foster the association's agenda, which ultimately is making money and retaining power.

The association has its hands in everything: drugs (both controlled substances and pharmaceuticals), guns, prostitution, professional sports, cars. If there is a way to make money—or take money—they find it. If a congressman wants to snort cocaine off of a sixteen-year-old's ass, the *gentiluomini privati* arrange and organize it—and cover it up. If a senator wants to hunt some human prey in the wilds of the Nezperce or Kootenai National Forest, the *gentiluomini privati* arrange it. If a nonmember of any significant power or influence has dirt, they expose it or cover it up, depending on the price and the effect on the association's agendas. Even if a member, say from Chicago, has a grudge and a perfect game needs to be sabotaged on the last out, it can be arranged.

The association runs up and down the east coast from Boston to DC and has pockets of influence in Miami and Chicago. The man in charge is Johnny Conti out of Boston. Johnny has large eyebrows and shifty eyes. He is short but looks as if he was carved from granite. His nose is slightly crooked from having been broken multiple times. He has a bald spot over his right ear, the product of a scar. He always wears his mother's Saint Christopher necklace. Johnny is known by most as Johnny C. He is feared by all as Johnny Sauce.

The name Johnny Sauce came into use after Johnny murdered his own *leccacazzi* brother for sleeping with Johnny's girl. Before Johnny snuffed out his brother, however, he reputedly forced his brother to eat a plate of pasta with a Bolognese sauce made from Johnny's unfaithful *puttana* ex-girlfriend, Lizella. After the incident, Johnny created a permanent reminder by getting a tattoo of a fork, tines down, twirling bloody spaghetti and piercing a bleeding human heart.

These days Johnny relied on others, especially Aeneid, to do his dirty work, but still nobody crossed him.

6

THE GOD-AWFUL ANNOYING BAP, bap, bap of the cheap hotel alarm clock woke Bret and Carwyn easily enough. They showered in turn and then made their way downstairs for breakfast. They had a full day ahead of them. They were going to the Vasa Museum to see an almost four-hundred-year-old Swedish warship, and they planned to tour the Royal Palace. For lunch they were going to brave a smorgasbord and eat themselves silly, if not sick. After that they were going to take an archipelago cruise. They thought they might venture out to take a second chance at getting into a nice club for a couple of drinks early, but they had decided to leave the next morning for Barcelona.

Different tourist information that they had read said that Stockholm was an archipelago made up of about thirty thousand islands and islets. They weren't sure they believed those numbers, but they still felt a cruise to be basically compulsory. The one they selected offered dinner. Neither Bret nor Carwyn was looking forward to any sort of a boat trip (or any more food) after the amount and variety of food that they packed away during their smorgasbord experience.

"I think I'm gonna puke, bro."

"Bret, don't even talk about puking or I will puke."

"You don't even know what half of what we ate was, so at least you'd get a second chance to identify it."

"Gross."

"Sorry, bro. Hey, have you noticed how well all the Swedes speak English?"

"Yeah, I have, actually, and it is wonderfully convenient."

"And have you noticed how stupidly long the words are?"

"Hadn't noticed that."

"Yeah, it's crazy, bro. The word for bathroom is something like pissingshittingwipingflushingroomatan."

"You are seriously a complete moron."

"I'm serious, bro—well, not about the word for bathroom. But did you notice the one when we were buying the aquavit in the liquor store?"

"No."

"*Rusdrycksförsäljningsförordningen* was the word. I think it means something like regulations for selling alcohol. You know what my favorite Swedish word is though?"

"No clue."

"*Slut*. I think *slut* means end or exit or closed or something like that. I saw a sign in a store window that said slut sale, seriously, *slut sale*. I mean, how awesome is that, bro?"

"Almost as awesome as your flip-flops."

"Fuck off."

The weather was perfect for a cruise, but soon after Bret and Carwyn sat down for dinner, they both realized what (regardless of the food quality) was going to be the highlight. Their server was otherworldly hot. After she had introduced herself as Karolina and taken their drink orders, Bret and Carwyn, as men often do, instantly commenced their discussion of her physical appearance. Carwyn was actually the first to comment: "Holy shit, now there is your bikini team right there, Bret."

"No kidding, bro. She is one of the hottest women I have ever seen—in person, of course."

"We should definitely talk to her. I mean besides ordering."

"Car, *you* should talk to her. I mean, did you see her rack?"

"Her rack? Man, did you see her eyes? And her dimples were adorable—okay, that sounded a bit lame—but yes, I also noticed that she is entirely well put together."

"Adorable? Well put together? Car, you're a pussy, bro. And you don't just sound lame; you sound like you belong in fucking *Brokeback Give-it-to-me-sweet-up-my-ass Mountain*."

"You're ignorant, and I am not a pussy. I just notice things other than a woman's breasts. I mean, I sure noticed her legs. They were near perfect."

"So you gonna talk to her?"

"We'll see."

When Karolina came back with their beers and asked if they were ready to order, Carwyn ordered the grilled salmon with prosciutto, and

Bret ordered the lingonberry duck confit. In addition to her electric blue eyes, perfectly placed and proportioned dimples, and her shoulder-length, slightly wavy, windblown blonde hair, Karolina had actress-caliber teeth that, with her thick and pouty lips, completed a perfectly sultry come-hither smile. She had one of those almost petite noses, curved in just the right way to make you doubt your chances. She was tall with milk-smooth skin and just the right amount of feminine muscle tone.

About two minutes after taking Carwyn and Bret's orders, Karolina came back with two small plates. On each was a piece of toast topped with a slightly pinkish creamy substance.

"It is called *skagenöra*. It is a typical Swedish appetizer. I thought you might like to try it. The main ingredients are shrimp, mayonnaise, dill, lemon juice, and onion."

"Does it come with our meals?" Bret asked.

"Well," Karolina said, cutting a deft, barely perceptible, glance from Bret to Carwyn and back, "it does tonight."

"Thank you."

"*Tack så mycket*," added Carwyn.

"*Nöje*, it is my pleasure. Do you need anything else right now?"

"I think we have everything we need for now."

Bret gave Carwyn an incredulous look: "*Tack så mycket? Tack så-fucking-mycket?* Are you fucking kidding me? Talk so puke-it is more like it. You just had to one-up me there, didn't ya, bro, throwing out the Swedish pleasantries."

"I wasn't trying to one-up you, jackass. I was being polite."

"Well, shit, I think it worked. Did you see that look she gave you?"

"She didn't give me a look."

"She sure as shit did, bro, when she told us that because she found you so dreamy she was giving us free Swedish deviled toast."

"That doesn't even make any sense, and it's actually pretty good. You should try yours."

"Car, you're missing the point. You *have* to talk to her now. I mean, 'it does tonight,'" Bret said, doing his best impression of a super hot Swedish waitress coyly speaking English.

"I might."

"Might? You are a gay, homo pussy. A stank and sandy, gay, homo

24

pussy. And a fucking idiot." Then Bret tasted his appetizer. "Not bad," he said, "but I bet she tastes better."

When Karolina brought the entrées, Bret and Carwyn each ordered another beer. She brought the beers and then checked on them a couple more times. After their meals, she cleared their plates and came back a couple minutes later with three dessert dishes.

"I did not know what you like, so I brought three."

"Thank you."

"What, no Swedish this time?" Karolina said with a wry smile.

"*Tack.*"

"That is better, and you are welcome," she said with a coy laugh. Then she walked off to the kitchen.

Proving that grown men can really be such schoolboys, Bret warned, "If you don't ask her out, I'm going to kick you square in the empty sack where your balls are supposed to be."

"Fine!"

Karolina returned with the bill. It listed their meals and only one beer each. The damage was three hundred crowns, about fifty bucks.

"Can you put this on two separate cards?" Carwyn asked.

"Yes. No problem."

She took the bill and walked off to run the cards.

"Last chance," Bret warned.

Karolina came back with the bill and placed it on the table between them.

"Karolina?" said Carwyn.

"Yes?"

"So, um, I have a question."

"Yes?"

"Well, my friend and I tried to get into like ten different clubs last night, but we couldn't get into a single one, and so we ended up freezing our asses off at the Ice Bar."

Karolina laughed. "And paying too much for drinks. The Ice Bar is a tourist"—she paused briefly to think of the word—"trap."

"Right, well, my question is, um, do you have any advice on how we could get into a more temperate place tonight?"

"Temperate?"

"Oh, sorry. That was a failed attempt at a really bad joke. Somewhere warmer. But what I really mean is a nicer place."

"You just have to dress and act the part. Dress and act cool without looking like you are acting cool—like you belong there."

"So that's it, huh? Dress up, act cool, and don't wear flip-flops?"

Karolina's reaction to the mere suggestion of wearing flip-flops to a Swedish club was priceless; she couldn't stifle her laughter. "*Ja*," she said, followed by a pause, "or you could come with me tonight."

Carwyn was a little caught of guard, but he tried to play it cool. "Well, that would make things easier. Are you going out tonight?"

"Yes. I am going tonight to see Timbuktu at Debaser. I work there part-time."

Bret interjected, "It's not like ABBA, is it?"

"*Nej*, Timbuktu plays Swedish hip-hop music."

"And you can get us in?" asked Carwyn.

"Yes, but only one of you, so the other will have to stay home. You can do—how do you say it—paper, rock, scissors."

"What?" Bret scoffed.

"I am joking. I can get you both in with me, if you would like."

"Sure, it should be fun. So, should we call you, or what?"

Karolina took the receipt from the table and wrote down her phone number and her address. "Meet me here at ten o'clock. If you get lost, call me. See you tonight."

"See you tonight," said Carwyn. "By the way, I love your accent."

After Karolina made her way back to the kitchen, Bret looked mockingly at Carwyn and chided, "Car, bro, you are a fucking dumbass! I love your accent? What in the fuck is that? I mean, seriously, you were doing so well up to that point, making me proud. Now we'll be lucky if she's even at that address when we get there tonight."

"I'm a dumbass? Are you kidding me? You, you ethnocentric idiot, actually asked her if the music we would be going to see tonight was like ABBA. Really? Fucking *ABBA*? Just because you happen to know one Swedish band does not mean you have to flaunt that sparse knowledge by acting like some culturally ignorant hillbilly. *That* was dumb."

"Hillbilly? Whatever. I'm still proud of you, bro."

The boat pulled back up to the dock about fifteen minutes later. Bret and Carwyn both gave a casual wave to Karolina as they disembarked. She smiled and waved back; then she was out of sight.

When they got back to the hotel, Bret told Carwyn to shower first so he could have as much time as possible to get ready for his date.

Before they left the hotel, they took a couple swigs of aquavit—which turned into drinking almost half the bottle between them. They were out the door at 9:42 but didn't get a cab for several minutes, and they didn't make it to Karolina's place until 10:14.

"This sucks; you're an even bigger dumbass for not calling her. Why didn't you call her? She's probably already gone."

"I don't know. I just didn't, okay?"

"Car, bro, you're my friend, and I love ya, but you're the biggest damn stupid-ass chickenshit I know."

"Gee, thanks for your support."

They paid the cab driver and made their way to the door. Carwyn hesitated for a second, so Bret stepped in front of him and rang the doorbell. A guy over half a foot taller than both Bret and Carwyn opened the door. "*Tjena*."

"Uh, hello, is Karolina here?"

Karolina noticed Carwyn and Bret at the door and issued a polite command in Swedish for the tall man to let them in. Karolina introduced the Americans to the Swedes. There were two guys, including the large doorman, and two other girls in the house. Bret spent the entire time trying to ascertain if they were paired up. Bret was so subtle that Carwyn didn't even notice the interpersonal reconnaissance.

"So you finally arrived," Karolina said to Carwyn. "I did not think you were going to make it. We are to leave in ten minutes. Would either of you like a drink?"

"Please." Carwyn didn't know the Swedish word for please or he certainly would have used it.

Karolina returned to the kitchen and made drinks for Carwyn and Bret.

"Why did you not call? I thought you were not going to come."

"Honestly, I don't know. Sorry."

"It is okay, you are here now. Enjoy your drink, and then we are going to leave. Tonight will be fun."

The way Karolina smiled when she said "you are here now" gave Carwyn a nice tingly feeling. He thoroughly enjoyed his drink. Bret had two. They chatted somewhat uncomfortably with the rest of the crowd for a few minutes and then made their way out.

Once at Debaser, true to her word, Karolina got Bret and Carwyn right in. They didn't even have to pay the cover charge. The place was crowded, but the group made their way to the bar to order drinks. They were barely able to order and get their drinks before the music started and the crowd went mildly crazy. As they endeavored to make their way from the bar, the group got separated.

Karolina grabbed Carwyn's hand and pulled him off toward a corner of the club. Bret got stuck with the other Swedes he hardly knew. The music was upbeat. It was almost all in Swedish, but it was good. Carwyn and Karolina danced flirtatiously with each other. There was definitely some sexual tension.

A little after 1:00 a.m., Carwyn got a text from Bret: "Not a bad show. swedes were actually nice & fun but i got separated from them about 20 min ago. gonna head back 2 hotel. Good luck have fun but don't 4get we r flying 2 barcelona 2morow and need 2 get up earlyish 2 get ticks."

Carwyn replied simply, "Sorry we got separated karolina is awesome catch ya later."

A little before two in the morning, although the show wasn't over, Karolina leaned over to Carwyn's ear and said, "The show will be over soon. Would you like to go back to my house?"

"I would."

Without saying another word, she grabbed his hand, and they made their way to the exit. When they got outside, Karolina told Carwyn they could walk back to her place in about fifteen minutes. So they walked.

The air was crisp and cool, and the refulgent moon seductively illuminated clouds that looked almost like they had been painted into the sky. Karolina grabbed Carwyn's arm, and the pair began their walk back to her place. She still smelled good, and she somehow looked even sexier in the moonglow.

Although Carwyn had been with multiple girls (mostly in the context of monogamous, even if brief, relationships), he was not actually a big one-night-stand kind of a guy. That had always been Bret's MO. Carwyn didn't actively avoid one night stands; he just didn't go trolling for them like a lot of other guys.

After they had been walking for a few minutes, without planning it or even really knowing why he did it (perhaps the booze, perhaps the moonlight), Carwyn stopped Karolina in the middle of the sidewalk they had been promenading down and kissed her. She welcomed the kiss, kissed back, and then pulled away.

"My house is less than a kilometer ahead."

Carwyn knew that a kilometer was less than a mile but was unsure of just exactly how much less. He was, however, content to keep walking. So they continued walking, still arm in arm. They didn't talk, and now that they were away from the club, the night was quiet. In what seemed like no time at all, they were walking up to Karolina's door. There was a light on inside. Karolina retrieved her key and unlocked the door. Carwyn followed her in. Just inside, he noticed three other people sitting on the couch watching TV.

"*Hej, Karolina, hade du kul?*"

"*Hej, ja, jag hade kul.*"

One of the three said something else in Swedish. Karolina's reply elicited some laughter, after which the three interlopers (as Carwyn viewed them) made one final comment. Carwyn couldn't even begin to know what to think. He could feel the warm sting of what might be embarrassment coloring his cheeks, but he didn't care all that much. *At least it isn't Karolina's parents. That would be awkward.*

"What did you just say to them, and what did they say?"

Karolina smirked. "Nothing."

"So they must be your roommates?"

"*Ja.*" And with that, she led him to her room. It was decorated stylishly but moderately. The only seemingly out of place item was a poster of some Swedish soccer player on the wall. Upon seeing it, Carwyn laughed out loud. The resemblance was striking.

"What?"

"Your roommates said I looked like this guy, didn't they?"

A cute laugh escaped from Karolina's sexy lips. "*Ja.*"

"And then what did you say?"

A wide smile surfed across Karolina's face. "I said, yes, a little, but we will see if he can score like Ljungberg can."

"You actually said that? You didn't say that, did you?"

Karolina chuckled probably one of the sexiest chuckles in the history of chuckling and said, "Yes, and then they said Ljungberg has retired from Swedish football, so he cannot score like he used to."

"Great."

"Shhh," she said. "I did not tell them I would give you all night to score as much as you wanted in whatever positions you preferred."

Another soccer reference, but that one shut Carwyn up. His jaw may very well have dropped wide open, but absolutely no sound whatsoever came out. Karolina shut her bedroom door and stripped down to her simple but exquisitely sexy underwear. If there was a woman that could literally make a man drool, Karolina was that woman.

She turned on a small lamp and turned off the overhead light. Next she went over to her laptop and put on some ambient techno music. *Good choice*, thought Carwyn. *No words to distract us.* Karolina walked back over to Carwyn and helped him out of his clothes. Then she removed her underwear, and they stood in front of each other stark naked for a moment. It was the most natural first-time-naked-with-a-new-girl experience Carwyn had ever had. *Let the games begin.*

Karolina had not exaggerated the positions thing. They made use of her entire room for a combined six orgasms over the course of about two or three hours, and Carwyn made sure to watch as much of the action as he could in Karolina's dresser mirror. Four of the orgasms were enjoyed by Karolina, but Carwyn actually had two. During his second (the miraculous sixth overall), Karolina whispered into his ear, "*Mål.*"

Then Karolina reached across Carwyn's body to turn out the light. Carwyn and Karolina both fell asleep relatively quickly without any kissing or cuddling. They had earned some sleep.

7

CARWYN WOKE TO LIGHT darting in through Karolina's window and around the edges of her curtains. He looked at her clock: 9:58. "Shit." Carwyn gently shook Karolina awake.

"*God morgon mästaren*," she said, unawkwardly and only slightly sleepily.

"Good morning ... um, hey, I really hate to do this, but I really have to get going. My friend Bret and I are leaving for Barcelona today, and I should have been back to our hotel already."

"You are going to be in trouble," Karolina said playfully.

"Yeah, I might actually," Carwyn replied with a laugh.

"I can call you a taxi."

"That would be great." *Was this the perfect woman or what?* he thought. But Carwyn knew she wasn't. She was super hot and insanely good in bed. She was nice—and she didn't have morning breath. But what was that saying he had heard somewhere before? It takes more than just sugar and flower to bake a cake. Something was just ... missing. Carwyn had no idea what. Maybe it had nothing to do with *her* at all.

Carwyn went into the bathroom to pee and splash some cold water on his face. His bathroom experience was far too eventful, because when he peed, it came out in not just two but three divergent streams. He had to wipe up after himself when he was done. While he was cleaning up his mess, Karolina went downstairs to call a cab.

After examining himself in the mirror and wondering how it is that some people are able to look at a person and tell when they have had sex for the first time in a while, Carwyn made his way downstairs. No longer embarrassed by the night before, Carwyn did not give Karolina's roommates a second thought. When he got downstairs, Carwyn saw that Karolina had quickly prepared him some toast with orange marmalade and a cup of coffee. He hoped it was strong.

"The taxi should be here soon."

"Great. Thank you—and thank you for the toast and coffee."

"Would you like some yogurt or anything else?"

"No, thank you. This is perfect."

Carwyn sat eating his toast and drinking his strong-enough coffee in silence for a couple minutes.

"I do not think that I will see you again after today, but I had a very good time last night," Karolina half whispered.

"I did too. Walking in with your roommates waiting on the couch was definitely a bit of a surprise, but I guess I got over that pretty quickly."

"*Ja.* I would say you did. Have you left anything upstairs?"

"No, I didn't have anything to leave. Thanks for asking."

Outside, the taxi driver honked his horn. Carwyn quickly finished his coffee and stood up. Karolina stood and walked him to the door. As he was heading out, she tip-toed up to move in for a not so much awkward as somewhat superfluous good bye kiss. Carwyn fully accepted the kiss, and as it extended past the mere good-bye kiss point to an enjoyable but not particularly passionate kiss, Carwyn reached for his wallet.

The kiss seemed to end abruptly, as if a force of some kind had pulled them apart. The same force seemed to hang in the air like a gaseous weight that was pulling coldly at his shoulders. Carwyn opened his wallet and took out one of Bret's business cards.

"I'll be in Europe for several more days, so you can give me a call or send me an e-mail if you like. It's actually one of Bret's cards, but it's got my phone number and e-mail address on it. It's a US phone number, so ..."

"Okay. *Tack.*"

Karolina gave a smile as Carwyn showed the cabbie the address she had written down for him. Carwyn waved. Karolina waved. Then the taxi drove off, and before it had even turned off of Karolina's street, the space between them seemed infinite. Karolina was a super, incredibly sexy girl. She wasn't dumb. She wasn't snobby. She wasn't annoying. She was good in bed—*very* good in bed. But Carwyn knew that he would never see her again. Somewhat paradoxically, while he wasn't bothered by the assumption that he would never see Karolina again, he *was* bothered by the fact that this assumption didn't bother him.

In the cab, Carwyn finally got around to checking his phone. There were two voicemails from Bret. The first was from 8:21 a.m. Bret had simply said, "Wake up, dick." The second voicemail, left at 9:30 a.m, was a bit lengthier: "Hey Car, you big fucking lazy pimp-daddy dumbass, we're leaving for Barcelona today, in case you don't recall. And we were gonna head to the airport early since we didn't have tickets yet. Well anyway, fuck-breath, I'm actually at the airport now. I didn't check out of the hotel, so I hope you get there in time to do that, you retard. I decided to go ahead and book a flight for myself for ten-forty. I got you a flight too, for two-ten this afternoon. *Your* flight is on Ryan Air, so good luck with getting your suitcase on the plane. Anyway, bro, I *am* fucking annoyed right now, but I'm not mad. That bitch was crazy hot and her legs were a mile long, so I would have worn myself out on that ass too. But you better catch your fucking flight so we can party it up in Barcelona tonight. I hope you get this soon and hurry your ass up."

Carwyn had to smile at the ridiculousness of Bret's message, but regardless of the seeming indifference he felt as he left Karolina behind, he was definitely annoyed by Bret referring to her as a bitch. *Strange*, he thought.

When Carwyn got back to his room, he quickly showered and packed. He was out of the room and back at the front desk to check out by eleven thirty. He had the pleasant woman at the front desk call a cab for him. When he got to the airport and tried to check in for his flight, he found out that his suitcase was indeed too big to take on the plane, and Ryan Air did not check luggage. Carwyn got his ticket anyway and made his way to a store that sold luggage. He purchased a backpack large enough to cram most of his stuff into but small enough to carry on the plane.

Carwyn thought about the joy he would get from punching Bret when he saw him next, but then he remembered that he was the one who was late. Well, maybe he would punch Bret anyway. And then his flight was delayed.

The hour delay seemed to last about five, and Carwyn forgot to call Bret. As soon as he landed, just before seven o'clock, he turned on his phone and saw that Bret had called. He didn't bother to listen to the message but immediately called Bret back. Bret would probably be the one doing the punching now.

"You are a douche," was Bret's immediate comment.

"Bret, man, the flight was delayed."

"Are you serious?"

"Yes. Anyway, I'm here now, so what's the plan?"

"Well, since I didn't know what your dumb ass was doing or when you were gonna get here, I already did some shit. I met a couple of Americans that have been here a few days, and they told me that although the *porto olympico* is a bit cheesy, it has a ton of bars and small clubs and is worth a visit."

"Fine, where are you now?"

"I'm heading back to the hotel. Where are you?"

"Just landed."

"Well, hurry the fuck up, bro!"

Bret gave Carwyn the address for the hotel, and Carwyn began his trek. He took a train and then walked about two miles. It took him over half an hour to get there. When he finally made it to the room, he was exhausted. Some backpacker he would make. He knocked on the door, and Bret opened it with a beer in hand.

"Well, glad you could finally make it, partner," Bret said, speaking with some kind of cowboy accent.

"Are you drunk?"

"No, just buzzed. Hey, where'd your suitcase go?"

"Oh, yeah, I forgot to mention that on the phone. I couldn't take it on the plane, so I had to cram everything into this backpack. You prick."

"Oh right, I'm a prick. Silly me; I forgot. Suitcases were a bad idea anyway, bro, if we're gonna be taking the train a bunch. You're probably better off."

"Maybe so."

"Hey so let me tell you, La Sagrada Familia—I toured it while waiting on your dumb ass. Enigmatic masterpiece by Antoni Gaudi. They'll never finish it. That's part of the draw, you know? It's beautiful, unique, perfectly imperfect in its incompleteness. Because of its unique architectural style and its drawn-out, at times completely halted construction, there's a touch of mystery to it. If you think about it, this church is the very quintessence of what sustains the human spirit. Without a little mystery or wonder, there's nothing to live for. If you know all the answers, then there are no questions to ask; and without questions, there is no curiosity or interest or purpose or motivation or will to live."

"Dude, are you high?"

"Probably; the Americans I met gave me some weed."

"So you're drunk *and* high?"

"No, no, man, I am very mildly buzzed, and only just a little high, and they cancel each other out anyway."

"Weed and alcohol do not just cancel each other out."

"Well, anyway, whatever. Can't a brotha philosophize every now and then without getting chastised for being high? Shit, a really high person wouldn't make the brilliant observation I just made. But whatever, get your ass ready, yo."

8

So there are good cops, and there are bad cops—and there are dirty cops. To be fair, the majority are probably good, doing their duty and upholding the law. There are those who might bend the rules for the utilitarian sake of justice—using excessive pressure or even coercion to obtain confessions and gather other information, testing the limits of the fourth, fifth, and sixth amendments to the Constitution of the United States. These rule-bending officers of the law are rather readily accepted by most as a necessity of the modern world, doing what it takes to keep the streets safe and put the bad guys behind bars. The bad cops just fuck shit up.

Then there are those cops that bend the rules and even break the law for their own personal gain. They take bribes, look the other way, tip off criminals, promote prostitution, profit from drugs that they confiscate from one dealer or user and then sell back to another. These cops abuse the very power bestowed upon them by society not to pursue justice but rather to promote certain crimes, protect certain criminals, and profit from both their associations with criminals and their own illegal activities.

As it is with cops, it is with doctors, lawyers, politicians, teachers, mechanics, et cetera. There are always the good, the bad, and the dirty. We always hope that when we have the need for a doctor, lawyer, mechanic, or even a police officer, we are fortunate enough to get a good one.

Sergeant Kieran Lorenz was not only a bad cop but a dirty cop, and in the interests of padding his wallet (partially to feed his two children and partially to feed his prostitute addiction), he had formed a coalition with three other cops who were all just as dirty as Lorenz. What made Lorenz's little outfit dangerous was that its members, in addition to being immoral, were impatient and impulsive—and they tended to fuck things up (they certainly fucked things up for Bret

Hightower). But since the foursome had occasionally proven useful, they all remained in the *gentiluomini privati*'s pocket—meaning, for the most part, that they remained protected.

9

THE OTHER AMERICANS BRET had met had given accurate information; the *porto olympico* was a bit cheesy, with tons of bars each trying harder than the next to get you to come in. But there was a good crowd, there was variety, and the music, for the most part, was good. Bret and Carwyn meandered in and out of a couple different bars and had a few drinks before they found one that was worth staying in for at least a little while. They were making fresh mojitos and caipirinhas, and the crowd was populated with attractive women. Carwyn had three or four liberally poured mojitos, and then, with liquid courage, he walked up to a group of three girls and introduced himself to one.

"Hi. I'm Carwyn."

"I'm Jessica."

Another American. Imagine that. "So, Jessica, are you a drinker or a dancer?"

"What?"

Carwyn leaned in closer. "I said are you a drinker or are you a dancer?"

"Oh. Um, well, both, I guess."

"Well, I see you have a full drink, so do you want to dance?"

She cut her friends a glance, and they gave subtle return glances of approval. As Carwyn and Jessica made their way to the dance floor, Bret walked up to the two remaining girls.

Jessica definitely danced differently from Karolina. Meanwhile, Bret was attempting to smooth talk Megan and Courtney. He ascertained that they were

Juniors at Iowa, ages twenty and twenty-one, but both of legal drinking age in Spain.

"So where are you from?" they asked simultaneously. Bret wondered what would work best. He worked up a slight accent. Never mind that he had already been talking to them for a minute or two without any accent or conjured persona.

"I am from Pamplona España, but I go to med school at UCLA."

Bingo. Jackpot. They both ate it up. Neither girl registered the accent switch, but it was Courtney who took the lead in the conversation.

"Oh really? Cool. How do you like America?"

"Well, I had visited New York with my *familia,* and I liked it. California is very different. But I like it for most part."

"For the most part?"

"*Si.* The cars are too big and there are a lots of the rude people." Of course Bret strategically failed to mention that he actually drove a mammoth, gas-guzzling SUV.

"Oh, you think so, huh?"

"I do not think you two *hermosas* are rude."

"Thank you. You know, your English is really good."

Bret didn't miss a beat, and he was glad he wasn't overdoing it with his preposterous accent.

"I started to learn the English when I was eight. Then I spent semester abroad in DC, and I have lived in California now three years."

"Oh, right! Well what kind of medicine do you want practice?"

"I want to be a *medico del amor*—a love doctor." If Bret hadn't been pretending to be Spanish, the two hot Hawkeyes might have just up and walked off right then and there, but he was pretending to be Spanish, so they ate it up along with all the other bullshit Bret was spouting.

"A love doctor?"

"Yes, this is medical school joke, I guess. I want to be a heart surgeon."

"Oh wow. That must be really hard."

"*Si, pero* I am *muy bueno* with my hands." That elicited a wry smile and a giggle from both of the girls. Bret felt like this was just way too easy.

"What are you ladies drinking, *esta noche?*"

"Vodka and cranberry juice."

"You take shots? That is a very American thing, no?"

"Sure, let's do it," said Courtney.

"What you like?"

"Well, since you offered, we assume you're buying, so you can pick."

"You are sure? If I to pick, I pick tequila."

"That's fine with us. Right Megan?"

The girls gave each other a nod.

"Sure."

So Bret inched to the bar and ordered the shots. *Finally*, he thought, *taking five years of Spanish might prove useful.* He handed the girls their shot glasses and, having always been impatient, thought this was as good a time as any for the first real test.

"So, I give toast. It is of my friend from Texas. He make all the time, and he have explain me … here is to honor: to have honor and to get honor; to keep honor; and if you cannot come in her, come honor."

Bret waited to see if the girls approved, which it seemed they did, or at least—if they got it—they didn't disapprove. They all took their shots and sucked the juice from their limes.

"So you ladies want 'nother shot or you want dance?"

"Another shot first, then let's dance."

Bret ordered another round of shots, and then they hit the dance floor.

Courtney was definitely digging him, but Megan seemed a hint aloof.

At the other end of the dance floor, Jessica was really starting to raunch up her dancing. She was rubbing and touching Carwyn all over, but he was only moderately interested in her advances.

"So where are you from, Carwyn?"

"Maryland."

"Oh." She definitely seemed disappointed.

"Yeah, sorry. My name only sounds Welsh because of my great-grandfather. I was named after him."

"I'll still fuck you though."

Carwyn was caught off guard. "Excuse me?" He thought, *It must be the alcohol talking.*

"Don't you want me?"

"Um, well, I don't *not* want you, but I hadn't really thought about it."

"Whatever."

She began to walk off. *What the fuck?* Carwyn stood for a moment in a mild state of shock and then realized he should make sure that Jessica found her friends—and then see if he could find Bret.

While Carwyn was being propositioned on the dance floor, Bret was thinking about how he was going to do some propositioning of his own. Just as he was going to make a move on Courtney, she excused herself, presumably to visit the ladies' room.

"So, Megan, you do not seem to be having as much fun as Courtney. *Que pasa?*"

"She always hooks up with all the guys we meet. She's more outgoing, better looking, and the guys always go for her—just like you are."

Bret hadn't expected such honesty, but tequila had a way of eliciting the truth. He figured he could use it to his advantage.

"I wasn't going for anybody. There is enough of me to share. She was talking to me, so I talk back. I think you are way hotter, *la más bella.*" *Let's ride this train and see where it goes*, Bret thought.

"You do?"

"*Si. Absolutamente.*" He didn't. "I have wanted you since I saw you. I would take you right here and right now, *aquí y ahora.*"

"Right here?"

"*Si.* In this crowd, I bet we could find a place."

"I don't believe you at all," Megan said.

"Well' there is only one way to find out."

Bret extended his hand. When Megan took it, Bret began to scour the bar for a darker, more secluded corner. When they got to where Bret thought was the best spot, Bret backed up to the wall and pulled Megan up to him. Then he quickly and aggressively turned her around so that she was facing away from him. In her current state of tequila-heightened arousal, this show of sexual aggression (which may well have annoyed or turned off a sober Megan), made her want it even more.

"You feel that? You still think I am joking?"

"I do feel it, but I still don't believe you."

Bret unzipped his pants with one hand as he reached up Megan's skirt to pull her panties to the side. There weren't any.

"Well, that will make things easier."

"If you don't chicken out."

Bret grabbed himself with one hand while pulling her back onto him. Then he used his hand to guide himself to the exact spot he wanted to be. Megan let out a muted gasp but then began to rock and grind on him.

"I guess you believe me now," he said, his accent waning.

"I guess I do," she said as she continued to move on him subtly.

After about two or three minutes, Courtney spotted them and made her way in their direction. Bret spotted her too, pulled out, and quickly went to work maneuvering himself back into his pants.

"There you two are."

"We've been here the entire time," Megan said.

"Okay, bitches," said Courtney, "I think it's about time we do more shots."

"Lead the way," said Bret.

Courtney turned and headed in the direction of the bar. Bret hung back just a step so he could ask Megan, "You want to continue this at my hotel?"

"You've got to finish what you started, mister."

"What about Courtney?"

"She's a big girl; she can take care of herself."

"She can't come?"

Silence. Bret thought he had ruined his opportunity, and if there was any balance in the universe, he surely would have.

"What, I'm not good enough for you?"

"No, you are, but wouldn't you like Courtney to see that I want you more?" *I am actually a genius*, he thought to himself, and he couldn't hold back the smirk.

Silence.

"Let's just see what happens."

At the bar, Bret ordered six shots, two for each of them. *We'll see, my ass!* They downed the shots, and then Bret suggested to Courtney, "Let's get out of here." The three of them left the bar and headed to where they could hail a cab. In the cab, Bret sat between the two girls, and his hands quickly made their way between the legs of both Courtney and Megan. Neither complained.

When they got back to the hotel, Bret put his brilliant-but-perhaps-despicable plan into action. He walked with Courtney between him and Megan. Once in the room with the door locked, he instantly began to make out with Courtney. He removed her top, and then he went for her skirt. She *was* wearing underwear. When he thought the time was right, he stepped away from Courtney and got Megan out of her clothes.

∗   ∗   ∗   ∗

Jessica and Carwyn had passed the others in the bar without seeing them. Carwyn tried to call Bret but got no answer. Jessica texted both of her friends. She got a response from Courtney: "Just got 2 hotel w hottt spanish med student."

"Figures."

"What?"

"My friends ditched me for some Spanish guy."

"You want me to walk you back to your hotel?"

"That would be nice. We're staying just a few blocks away."

Carwyn walked with Jessica back to her hotel and up to her room. She was pretty drunk. When she finally managed to get her key out of her purse, drop it, pick it up, and then insert it into the slot in the door, Carwyn expressed his sympathy. "I'm sorry your friends left without you. You sure you're gonna be okay?"

"Yeah, I'll be fine. They're just dumb sluts anyway."

"Okay, Well, have a goodnight." *Incredible*, he thought. *The twenty-first-century woman never ceases to surprise and amaze. Shit, us twenty-first century men aren't any less messed up.*

Carwyn made his way down the hall to the elevator, incredulous. He could not believe that Jessica had actually called her two friends dumb sluts after telling him that she would fuck him in the middle of the bar.

When Carwyn got back to his hotel room, he immediately noticed two naked girls passed out on one bed and Bret on the other. *Holy shit! It's the other girls from the bar. Spanish guy, my ass! Bret,* he thought to himself, *if you weren't my best friend … well, the floor it is.* Carwyn used some of his clothes to fashion a kind of make-shift pallet and pillow. It served him just fine. It had been a long day, and even with his involuntary arousal from seeing two attractive, completely naked girls just steps away from him, Carwyn quickly fell asleep.

∗   ∗   ∗   ∗

Carwyn was roused early in the morning by a bit of a kick to the face. He looked up to a glass-smooth shaved crotch.

"Owe," Courtney said as she tripped over Carwyn's head. She looked down at him and said, "Who the hell are you?" She must have still been drunk, because she didn't seem to mind being completely naked in front of a random stranger.

"I'm Cheech Marin's best friend."

"What?"

Carwyn didn't respond but rather asked, "Who are *you*? And what are you doing naked in my boyfriend's hotel room?"

"Your boyfriend?"

"Yes," Carwyn said, adding a bit of flamboyance now, "my boyfriend. You didn't sleep with him, did you? He so always hits on girls when he gets drunk."

There was a moment of silence that was awkward for her and hilarious for him, but then Carwyn caved. "Just kidding."

"Wait, what? Is he really your boyfriend, or what?"

"Nope, but he is engaged to be married."

Courtney quickly surveyed the room and pieced together her outfit from the night before.

"Have you seen my friend?"

"Who?"

"My friend Megan. She was here with me."

"I haven't seen anybody except you. I was asleep until you kicked me in the face."

"Oh, right. Well, I am sorry about that."

"No worries."

"That little tramp must have gotten up before me and started her walk of shame without even waking me up. Bitch!"

The incredulity from last night ratcheted up a notch. Maybe it was an Iowa thing, but these girls were *insane*. Courtney grabbed her purse and headed for the door. Carwyn was wondering what went through a girl's mind as she made the walk of shame when, out of the silence, Bret asked, "Are they gone, bro?"

"So you're alive. How long you been awake?"

"Just woke up now, really. Heard the door shut."

"Sure you did. So you must have had fun last night."

"You missed out, bro."

"Bret, do you actually *remember* last night?"

"Fortunately enough for me, I do."

"What the hell, man?"

"What?"

"Did you seriously trick those girls into thinking you were Spanish for the purposes of having a threesome? What about Rebecca?"

"I actually thought I overplayed it, but it was classic, bro. And I'm just sowing my wild oats. You did the same thing with Karolina."

"I didn't lie to Karolina or get her drunk. And there's just one other small detail you seem to be overlooking: you're engaged. Your oat-sowing days are over. It should be all reaping for you from here on out."

"What Rebecca doesn't know can't hurt her."

"Unless you pass on whatever diseases you pick up."

"Whatever. Wanna know what happened?"

"You know, I'll just leave it to my imagination."

"Suit yourself, bro."

"Bret, I'm going back to sleep—in my damn bed this time."

"Good idea."

10

AN EXTREMELY SHARPLY DRESSED businessman strode confidently down the street. Today he was in Kraków, but any given day of any given week you could find him conducting business in any number of European cities. The businessman had once worked for a highly successful corporation. Since he had invested wisely, he had decided to give up his cushy job.

Now he was his own boss. He had no permanent employees, but he retained any number of distinctly skilled individuals from time to time as the need arose.

He lived in Munich, where his most spacious home and the garage for his small but steadily growing automobile collection were located. He had moderate homes in Riga and Moscow. He even had a small apartment in Tokyo. He relished the time he got to spend in Tokyo—something about the Japanese way of life appealed to him.

The businessman had the aura of a successful entrepreneur about to conclude yet another lucrative transaction. He had brokered around five or six deals a year for the past four years, with profits ranging from 500,000 to 6.5 million euros per deal. He'd averaged a profit of approximately twelve million dollars a year for the last four years. His methods were definitely unorthodox. Some might have called them cold, if not cold blooded. Empathy, however, had been the downfall of many otherwise talented businessmen.

The businessman had already concluded two successful deals this year and was about to seal another. Recently, on more than one occasion, he had thought about getting out of the business at year's end. He didn't really need the money, but a significant part of him particularly—even if perversely—enjoyed his line of work.

Looking back on it, he had gotten into his current line of work more for the thrill than the money. It couldn't even be called work, really—more like play. The businessman took his untraceable cryptophone from his pocket. The technology in the expensive, nonretail market phone made his calls untraceable and uninterceptable, regardless of the phone being used on the other end. He dialed the number for his latest business partner and pressed the send button.

11

CARWYN AND BRET WOKE again at a quarter past eleven. They got ready in silence, but by the time they were heading out, any awkwardness between them had faded. They checked out of their hotel before leaving but were able to store their luggage for the day. Wearing T-shirts and swim trunks and carrying towels, they made their way directly to Las Ramblas to eat, drink, and people watch.

Their plan was to relax on the beach all day and take the ferry to Rome. Then, to further take things easy, they would spend the following day in Rome sightseeing followed by a full five-course Italian meal and absolutely no all-night clubbing. Neither one of them was twenty-one or twenty-two any more.

Las Ramblas was a people-watching oasis. There were all types of people strolling up and down the street. There were street performers galore. Carwyn and Bret sat down at an outdoor café and ordered seafood paella and two sangrias. When they got the bill, they could tell they were paying a little extra for the privilege of people watching. The sangrias were twenty-five fucking euros each.

Stuffed and a little buzzed from the sangrias, they made their way to the beach, where they stayed for two or three hours.

*   *   *   *

The Grimaldi Eurostar departed at 6:00 p.m. for Rome. Bret and Carwyn splurged on an inner cabin for seventy-five euros apiece. They hadn't checked the travel time before purchasing their tickets or setting off.

"Fifteen hours? Shit, we could have flown for cheaper and arrived in Rome like five times sooner."

"Well, at least we'll have plenty of time to catch up on sleep."

They arrived at Citivecchio ahead of schedule. When they got to Rome, they immediately checked into their hotel and then made their way to Vatican City. They saw the Swiss Guard, St. Peter's Square and Basilica, and the Apostolic Palace. Inside the Sistine Chapel, Bret asked, "Hey, what ninja turtle do you think you would be?"

"Bret, we are looking at possibly one of the world's greatest works of art, and you're seriously asking me what teenage mutant ninja turtle I would be? I don't know, maybe a combination of Raphael and Donatello."

"I think I would be Michelangelo."

After some more sightseeing, they made their final stop of the evening at the Museo della Pasta so as to work up a good two-hour appetite for their planned five or six-course Italian dinner.

It was five courses, and they found a moderately sized, not-so-moderately priced place just off the beaten path. They split two bottles of wine, and each ordered an *antipasto, primo, secondo, contorno,* and *dolce.* Bret had a sambuca and Carwyn a limoncello after their meal.

"I'm pretty sure that was the best meal I have ever eaten."

"By far."

It was dark when they left the restaurant, and they decided to check out the Trevi Fountain.

"Bro, we are so gay."

"What?"

"Well, we just had a romantic Italian dinner for two, and now here we are alone together at night at one of the most romantic fountains in the world."

Carwyn laughed and replied, "Bret, our dinner wasn't romantic; it was just good. And it's not like we're arm-in-arm sharing an evening stroll. There's nothing gay about sightseeing."

"So that's why our waiter put two spoons in each of our desserts?"

"Well, we tried some of each other's food, didn't we?"

"See? Gay. Very gay, bro."

"I never even gave it a thought."

"That's because you're gay," said Bret.

"Rebecca would beg to differ."

That comment earned Carwyn a quick, hard punch to the chest. Bret had a bad habit of responding to Carwyn's verbal jabs by punching him.

"Bret, after Barcelona, you can't keep pretending you care about Rebecca."

"I love Rebecca."

"You've got a funny way of showing it."

The long day of sightseeing, their gastronomic overindulgence, and two bottles of wine had all taken a toll. As planned, there was no bar or club hopping—and no sexual exploits.

The weather the next morning was beautiful. Carwyn and Bret got their start at about 10:00 a.m. after some espressos. After a full morning and afternoon of walking and sightseeing, Carwyn was craving some gelato.

"Are you serious, bro?"

"Yep. It should be a requirement for any non-lactose intolerant tourist."

"If you say so. Lead the way."

"I was planning on it."

They headed down Via di Ripetta and then across the Tiber River. Carwyn led them to Piazza Cavour by the Palazzo di Giustizia. They circled the Piazza without finding a suitable gelateria.

"You are way too fucking picky, bro."

Carwyn ignored Bret and took a couple smaller streets. They ended up walking for almost fifteen minutes and passing three or four places selling gelato before Carwyn found one he wanted to try. He looked over the selections for a minute or two before making eye contact to indicate he was ready to order. A woman acknowledged him and said, "Prego ... dimmi."

Carwyn replied, "Una coppa, due gusti ... una gusti di Nocciola, una gusti di Pistacchio." A moment later he had his cup jammed full of hazelnut and pistachio gelato. He was happy.

Bret ended up ordering a scoop of *cioccolato all'azteca*.

After Bret received his gelato, Carwyn thanked the woman and said to Bret: "I knew you'd end up getting some, how is it?"

Bret had just taken his first bite.

"Whoa."

"What?"

"Chocolate with cinnamon and hot pepper."

"Any good?"

"It's spicy, which is weird, but"—Bret took another bite—"it's actually damn good."

"Okay, you gotta let me try it."

"Bro, you got two scoops, plus I'm not big on sharing ice cream with another dude. It would be one thing if I got a cup, but licking another man's ice cream cone is just gay."

"Gay, gay, gay, blah, blah, blah ... I think *you're* gay."

"Oh, for fuck's sake, here, you big baby." Bret thrust his cone in Carwyn's face. Carwyn, feeling victorious, took a big bite.

They continued eating their gelato and turned down Via Paolo Mercuri. They had taken no more than a couple steps when Bret felt something brush against his ass. Instinctively, he turned around and swung. He made contact with the side of someone's face.

The would-be pickpocket fell hard to the ground. Bret took a half step toward the punk in order to kick him hard as he lay on the ground, but just as he cocked back his leg, he saw that the perpetrator was only a kid, no more than twelve or thirteen—hell, probably even younger. Bret didn't feel any guilt for the punch, because he figured the little shit deserved it, but he didn't follow through with a kick to the ribs.

Carwyn, who hadn't really seen what had happened, was just catching up on things. He quickly scanned the street. Carwyn knew that young pickpockets often worked for older kids or in pickpocketing rings and usually had someone who watched over them as they worked. Carwyn didn't notice anyone on the street that seemed to fit that description. In fact, the street was almost empty. The whole situation hadn't drawn much attention. The boy, who had a touch of blood on his nose and at his lip, looked up at Bret and said, "*Va fan culo.*" Then he scrambled to his feet and ran off.

Carwyn said, "I think that means 'go fuck yourself.'"

"What a little shit! I should have cracked his fucking ribs, bro."

"He didn't get your wallet, did he?"

"Hell no. But I dropped my motherfucking ice cream cone."

Carwyn laughed. "I'm sorry. You want to go back and get another one?"

"Nah, it's fine, fuck it. Let's just head back to the hotel so I can take a nap."

"A nap? Okay gramps."

They continued down Via Paolo Mercuri until Carwyn noticed a sign for the Museum of the Souls of Purgatory. "Let's check it out."

"You can't be serious, bro?"

"Sure, why not?"

"Okay," Bret relented, "whatever."

The museum was not much more than a small room next to a church, but it had about half an hour's worth of eerie displays of objects and photos said to show evidence of souls trapped in purgatory. Bret and Carwyn mulled around the museum separately. There was only one other person in the museum besides the lone curator. The museum had an early copy of Dante's Divine Comedy, reproductions of *The Trinity with Souls in Purgatory* by Corrado Giaquinto, *Purgatory* by Daniel Crespi, and other artwork depicting purgatory. It had urns and various objects said to belong to souls stuck in purgatory.

There were also several pictures that allegedly served as evidence of the great divine waiting area. Most of the pictures were of apparitions or unnatural light effects—overexposure, underexposure, or film defects, a skeptic might say. However, one picture in particular caught Carwyn's attention. The photograph, which looked to be about fifty years old, had been taken in a small living room.

In the picture there was a woman holding onto another photo of an old man. The man in the picture within the picture looked just like an elderly version of Carwyn. The resemblance was uncanny. The woman was dressed in black, and it appeared obvious to Carwyn that she was mourning the loss of her deceased husband.

There was also a younger man in the photograph, but he looked as if he was literally trapped in the floor of the small living room. This man looked as if he could have been Carwyn's darker-haired twin. The resemblance was so far beyond uncanny that Carwyn studied it for several minutes. He'd been told that he looked like certain celebrities or athletes before (the Swedish soccer player on Karolina's wall, for example), but never had Carwyn seen an image of someone who he actually thought he looked like.

As Carwyn leaned in for a closer look, the man seemed to reach out through the floor and then to literally, physically reach out through the picture itself as if attempting to touch Carwyn's face. Carwyn thought he felt a warm air current pass over him. He was so startled that he jumped back from the picture and nearly fell over. He bumped into an urn and had to react quickly to keep it from sailing to the floor and shattering. Bret looked over to him and tried not to laugh, as the museum obviously had a rather somber atmosphere.

"Get a little spooked there, buddy," he asked in a patronizing whisper, "or were you trying to release some poor bastard's soul from purgatory?"

"Very funny. Come look at this photo." Carwyn directed Bret's attention to the photograph of Carwyn's long-dead Mediterranean doppelganger trapped in the floor.

When Bret leaned in, Carwyn asked, "Do you see that?"

"See what?"

"In the floor."

"I don't see anything, bro."

"You don't see that?"

"No, I don't see anything in the damn fl—whoa!"

"You see it?"

"No, I still don't see anything in the goddamn floor, but the old guy in the picture that old lady is holding looks like he could be your grandpa."

"Yeah, I know. Kinda creepy, right? But are you sure you don't see anything in the floor?"

"Carwyn, if you ask me about that fucking floor one more fucking time, I swear to God, I—"

"Okay, fine, get out of the way. Let me see."

Carwyn leaned back in to the reexamine the photograph, but this time the floor was just a floor. "What the fuck?"

"What did *you* see?" Bret asked.

"Nothing, never mind."

"You seeing ghosts, bro? Tormented souls?"

"Something like that. You ready to get outta here?"

"Yeah. I think I've looked at every exhibit in this place."

"Me too."

Carwyn, quite unnerved by the haunting look-alike in the old photograph, and wondering if it meant something or if he was just hallucinating, wasted no time in heading for the door. As they were leaving, the old lady running the place looked at Carwyn and said, "Se l'hai visto, significa che il tuo cuore si trova in purgatorio. Solo l'amore vero può salvare la tua anima."

— 12 —

Carwyn's Brookline apartment was a small one bedroom on the first floor of a converted single-family dwelling. The apartment was one of four, but it had a private entrance. It was about two in the afternoon, and it was quiet.

The *gentiluomini privati* felt that the middle of the afternoon was the best time for certain undertakings. No lights would need to be turned on in the dark. Anything that might be witnessed would seem a little less out of the ordinary. Carwyn's unsuspected and uninvited but ultimately unobtrusive visitor, Aeneid, had all the right tools for the job: gloves, surgical booties, an old-fashioned locksmith's kit, a fully motorized lock picking device, a digital camera, an external hard drive, an assortment of bugs and GPS locators, and a selective-fire Glock C with a semi-automatic/fully automatic selector switch and no serial numbers, just in case.

The *gentiluomini* could have sent Lorenz or one of his jamook brethren, but they would not have been as thorough or as careful. In short, they would have fucked something up—again. Aeneid, dressed casually, ambled nonchalantly to Carwyn's front door and did not need to take any backward glances. The surrounding area had been fully reconnoitered in the walk up to Carwyn's apartment building.

Before getting to the door, Aeneid had fully diagnosed the handle and lock and determined the ideal lock-picking tool for the job. In an instant, Aeneid had deftly removed the requisite tool, picked the lock without as much as a single scratch, entered the apartment, and relocked the door behind her.

Carwyn's apartment had a combination kitchen and dining area with just enough room for a small table, a very small TV room, one bedroom, and one bathroom. Before looking for anything, Aeneid slipped on her surgical booties and then moved through the entire apartment taking pictures of every room. After taking about fifty pictures, Aeneid dissected and put back together each room one by one.

First she searched the kitchen: every drawer, every cabinet. Every open jar, can, bag, box, and tub was examined. The refrigerator, the oven, the microwave, and the shitty little dishwasher were looked through. The trash can was completely emptied out. The trash was rifled through and then re-disposed of. There was nothing in the dining area to search, so next up was the TV room.

Every item of furniture was searched, including in and under every cushion. Every single DVD case was opened, every DVD tested to make sure it was actually the original DVD. Aeneid was thankful that Carwyn did not have an extensive DVD collection but bummed that there wasn't a single sex tape hidden among the action flicks and romcoms; those were always a perversely pleasant surprise. After checking the DVDs, she flipped through and shook out every magazine.

Aeneid proceeded next to the bathroom, leaving the bedroom for last. She searched the medicine cabinet and every other cabinet and drawer. Each and every jar, can, bottle, and tube in the room was scrutinized. Aeneid looked in both the toilet bowl and the tank. The bathroom was clean, just like the kitchen and the TV room. If there was anything to be found, it had to be in the bedroom.

Carwyn's bedroom was tidy and just large enough for a small computer desk. Aeneid searched the desk first: every box, every file, every piece of paper was examined. Aeneid moved on to the closet and looked in every shoe and every pocket of ever article of clothing. At the bed, she searched each pillow and lifted the mattress. She completely unmade the bed, searched it, and remade it to look exactly as it had before. Every square inch of Carwyn's bedroom was searched with the thoroughness of about ten dozen anxious children (along with their overly helpful parents) hunting through Carwyn's apartment for the last Easter egg on earth.

After searching each room, Aeneid copied the entire hard drive from Carwyn's laptop to an external device. She copied every memory card and flash drive. Not a single one was protected in any way. When the search was complete, Aeneid placed bugs in each room, a tracking device in Carwyn's laptop bag, and several more devices in various articles of his clothing.

When the last of the bugs and tracking devices were put in place, Aeneid used the multiple pictures taken in each room to double check that not a single item was out of place. Nothing was (although Carwyn would probably never have noticed). And with that, the job was done. Aeneid's exit was just as nonchalant as her entrance. Unless they heard it from Aeneid's own mouth, nobody would ever know she had been there.

13

SITTING AT A CAFÉ on Via Condotti, Bret and Carwyn were forced to make a decision. It turned out that they hadn't done the best planning job in the world. It was over eight hundred miles from Rome to Amsterdam by train. The duo decided to forgo a night out in Rome and get right on a train to Amsterdam, traveling through the night.

They would take the Eurostar Italia from Rome to Milan and eat dinner on the train. Next they would get on a much slower train to Basel, Switzerland. After that they would take yet another train to Brussels, Belgium. The plan was to stop in Brussels for some Belgian Beer in La Grand Place and to see some peeing baby statue. From there it would be on to Amsterdam, the Venice of the north.

Lunch in La Grand Place made Carwyn feel like he was in a James Bond movie. Bret and Carwyn both ordered Dubbel Abbey beers and ate meals that were a fusion of French and German cuisine. After their meals, they tried Belgian blonde ales and ordered Lambics for dessert. Carwyn ordered cherry and Bret tried raspberry.

"I'm not quite sure you can really call this dessert."

"They're sweet."

"Yeah, but they have more alcohol than most American beers."

"That's my kind of dessert, bro."

After they finished their "dessert," Bret and Carwyn walked around a bit before going to see that damn pissing baby.

"You know, I really thought that baby would be more impressive."

"Me too," agreed Carwyn.

From Amsterdam Centraal station, Bret and Carwyn took a taxi to their hotel. They were staying pretty much at the edge of the red light district's very heart. After they checked in and dropped off their luggage, Bret convinced Carwyn to hit up the coffee shop scene.

They walked around for about ten minutes before Bret decided on a place. Bret was almost as particular about his weed as Carwyn was about gelato. Carwyn sat down at a table and let Bret do the purchasing. Carwyn knew almost nothing about marijuana. Bret arrived at the table with two bottles of water, a small baggie of something called witches' brew, and some rolling papers. He immediately set to work rolling two joints, exhibiting more care than a new mother holding her baby and more enthusiasm than a fat guy at an all-you-can-eat buffet. Carwyn had never rolled a joint, didn't care to learn how, and sure didn't see why the hell it took so long.

When Bret was done rolling three joints, he realized he needed a lighter and made his was back to the counter. He lit up and began smoking the joint as he made his way back to the table. When he got there, Bret lit Carwyn's joint and passed it to him.

It had been quite some time since Carwyn had smoked pot. The few times Carwyn had smoked, it had always been somebody else's idea. Carwyn had never purchased his own weed and owned no paraphernalia. He was pretty sure he had never even been all that high, let alone stoned. But he was in Amsterdam, he wasn't a prude, and Bret had paid for it; so Carwyn took the joint and inhaled. He inhaled just a bit too much and had to stifle a fit of coughing, finally suppressing it by chugging over half his bottle of water.

"Easy there, killer," cautioned Bret. He was almost finished with his first joint.

"Thanks for your concern, Scooby Doobie. Sorry I don't have quite the vacuum lungs that you do."

"It's all good, bro."

"So," asked Carwyn, "what do you want to do this evening?"

"Well, we didn't go out in Rome, so I'd like to do that—oh, and go to the weed museum."

Bret, who had blazed through his first joint, finished his second joint at about the same time Carwyn finished his first. Carwyn didn't feel anything, but he could tell that Bret had a moderate high going. This seemed backward to Carwyn. On the way out, Bret lingered in order to buy a space cake for Carwyn.

"I got you a present," Bret said as he met up with Carwyn out on the street.

"Oh gee, thanks. If you're trying to get my high, this sure isn't gonna do it."

"Just eat it, bro."

As they walked down Lange Neizel toward Oudezijds Achterburgwal, Carwyn unwrapped his space cake and took a bite.

"Damn, this thing is delicious. It isn't gonna get me high though. Sorry, bud." He added, "Pun intended," and laughed out loud at his own lame joke. *Shit*, he thought, *maybe I am getting high.*

After they walked through the entire weed museum in less than thirty minutes, Carwyn said to Bret, "Nine euros was a pretty high price to pay for that museum. Definitely a pothead tourist trap."

"Har har. Very funny, bro." Bret thought Carwyn's reference to a high price was another bad pun. It wasn't.

"So, Bret, you ready to check out the sex museum?"

"Yeah, sure, but after that, dinner time. Then it's slut time."

Carwyn tried to ignore Bret's slut comment, but he just couldn't let it go. "Bret, seriously, do you have any intention of *ever* being faithful to Rebecca once you're actually married?"

Instead of answering, Bret changed the subject. Carwyn didn't press him. What could he do, really? Bret was a constant reminder to Carwyn that sometimes friends were like family: you just had to take the good with the bad. Bret, notwithstanding his flaws, was not just Carwyn's best friend, but was like a brother to him.

They walked to the sex museum at Damrak 18. The entrance fee was only five euros. Both Bret and Carwyn were surprised to find that, unlike the small weed museum, the sex museum had three floors of exhibits. They spent an hour walking around, at times laughing out loud and at times groaning, while looking through the extensive collection of erotic paintings, pictures, objects, and recordings from different areas and cultures all over the world. It was like a complete global sex timeline.

When they were leaving, Bret said, "Okay, I'm starving. Let's eat."

They walked about a block before a FEBO caught Bret's eye. Before Bret ever even said a word, Carwyn noticed the almost prepubescent excitement that took a hold of him.

"You have *got* to be kidding me," preempted Carwyn.

"Dude, I've read about this place. Automated fast food. How much more stoner can you get? It's perfect for Amsterdam. This is just as much a part of the culture as coffee shops and women in windows."

"Okay. I mean, I guess we ate at a smorgasbord in Sweden and had a five-course meal in Italy; so some stoner fast food in Amsterdam is fine by me."

When they finished their meals, Carwyn wondered if they might pay later for what they had just eaten. As they began their walk back to their hotel, the sun was beginning its nightly descent, painting orange, yellow, pink, and even some purple across the sky with a masterful brush. Although the red light district never really stopped, with the setting of the sun and the impressionist transition from day to night, the area truly came to life. As Bret and Carwyn turned onto the Oudezijds Voorburgwal, they could see the array of world-famous windows tinted red and women selling the oldest service in the world.

"So I think we should see a sex show before going back to the hotel."

"Are you sure you really want to see a live sex show?"

"It's Amsterdam. We smoked in a coffee house, we ate at that weird FEBO place. We have to see a sex show too. It's just as compulsory as the rest of the shit we've done so far today."

"I guess you've got a point."

So they casually checked out a couple places, trying to avoid the salesmen at the various doorways describing how their shows were better quality and a better value than all the other sex shows in town. They settled on a place that cost twenty-two euros and included two free drinks. They went in and took their seats close to the front among a crowd full of Asian men and ordered their first free drinks.

"So what all exactly are we gonna see here?" Bret asked.

"You got me. To be honest, I have no idea what to expect."

After both acts of the show had concluded, and Bret and Carwyn left the "theater," Carwyn turned to Bret and commented, "So, uh, yeah … that was definitely different."

"Yeah, I'm not so sure what to think about that. I mean, I admit the first act or whatever you want to call it was entertaining, but the couple was definitely a bit weird."

"But now you've got another story for the ol' grandkids."

"Yeah, right. Anyway, do you think that was a real couple up there or just random performers?"

"That's a good question. I have no idea."

"Oh well. What type of place do you want to hit up tonight?"

"I dunno. I think the Leidseplein is the place to be at night, and we can just pick a place in that area."

"So who are we gonna be tonight?" inquired Bret.

"Huh?"

"What roles are we gonna take on, what's our angle going to be?"

"Angle for what?"

"To pick up da bitches, bro."

"Wow. You are unbelievable. I have no idea what our angle should be; that's your department. If it were up to me, I'd just as soon go with Bret and Carwyn, two guys who aren't douchebags."

"Weak sauce, bro."

"Bret, seriously, you are engaged to be married, and you are honestly talking about the lies we can tell to pick up women. That doesn't seem the least bit wrong to you?"

"Ladies and gentlemen: my friend the bitch-ass party-pooper."

"Bret, I'm all about meeting women—you know, for me—and having a good time, but I don't need a fake back story. And you already have a woman—a fiancée for Christ's sake. I mean, if Rebecca knew about half the shit you've been pulling on this trip, it would kill her. Hell, she would kill *you*. How is it that I never knew you were such a sleazeball?"

"Don't be melodramatic, bro. And I've got the perfect idea: we're big-time, high-paid lobbyists pushing for the legalization of marijuana in the United States. It's a good convo starter; it's not too far-fetched. You can improvise easily, and it evinces a certain degree of power while also being cool and rebellious. It's brilliant, if I do say so myself."

"Evinces power? Cool and rebellious? Are you shitting me? Do you hear yourself? You have seriously put way too much thought into this."

"Actually, I just came up with that. I'm a natural, bro."

"I'm not sure that makes it any better."

14

SERGEANT KIERAN LORENZ KNEW he had fucked up, and he was actually more than just a little bit scared that it might get him put in the dirt. As a solution, he suggested to Johnny Sauce that he and his guys take care of the problem by killing Bret Hightower along with all his close friends and family. It would have meant a lot of killing. Johnny was not in agreement with Lorenz's reckless solution.

"Think about it rationally, Lorenz. We cannot just go aroun' fuckin' killin' everyone this one guy fuckin' knows or that this one fuckin' guy may have come in contact wit'. The most prudent course of action is to determine who, if anybody, he's told about what he seen, and then eliminate those mugs only. As good as our resources—an' they ah fuckin' good—the biggah the body count we rack up, the greatah the chance of anothah fuckup or anothah witness. We'd have to go through this entiyah fuckin' process all the fuck ovah again. We want only the people with harmful information disposed of. If it turns out to be only one person, so be it. That would be even bettah, in fact, less of a fuckin' trail. Lorenz, ya stupid fucka, some people kill 'cause dey enjoys it, and while it's nice to have a person or two like that in your employ, we only kill outta necessity. When it *needs* to be done. *Capice?* In this way we're both feared an' respected. We'll continue to keep tabs on this poor fuckah, and, after we're done with a thorough inspection of his family, his friends, and his acquaintances, he and anyone else who knows more than he or she should know must, and will, be disposed of. It's as simple as that. We've got everything undah control."

Kieran most certainly didn't agree with Johnny, but Johnny was his boss. Johnny paid him, and Johnny could easily have him killed. So even though he wanted to take immediate action, Kieran decided to follow Johnny's instructions—orders really—and he would relay those orders to the rest of his guys.

15

THE AREA OF AMSTERDAM where Carwyn and Bret were headed was only about a mile or so away, so they decided to walk. There were a couple of larger groups of drunken Englishmen cavorting about, likely on stag nights. It was the hen parties Bret was interested in. As Leidsestraat became Leidesplein, the street became more populated. The first bachelorette group that Bret saw became his target. They were all wearing devil horns, and the bride-to-be was wearing a little white veil.

Bret marched right up to the group of eight women and introduced himself as Brent. Carwyn, who had followed along behind, was introduced as Aaron. Bret had informed Carwyn that he had picked the names because if either he or Carwyn slipped up with their aliases, the slip-up could be explained away easily as having been misheard.

Bret nonchalantly inquired as to the best place to go for drinking and dancing. The women, who were from Peterborough, England, responded that they were going to a club called Paradiso, and Bret finagled what was more or less an invitation for himself and Carwyn to accompany them.

Paradiso was housed in an old church, and there was a small line to get in. There was also a fifteen-euro cover charge. Bret's offer to pay the bachelorette's entry fee was graciously accepted. As they made their way in, one of the Brits yelled, "Let's get pissed," and the rest of the group responded with whoops of approval and agreement.

The club was pretty large, and a tech crew was making some final adjustments on the stage in preparation for the band. The women made their way directly up to the bar, followed by Bret and Carwyn. After ordering a couple beers for himself and Carwyn, Bret reengaged with a different member of the group. They chatted for five or ten minutes, and Bret was able to lay out his and Carwyn's false background story.

Meanwhile, Carwyn was making small talk with two other

members of the group. The women seemed as if they had already had several drinks. They were talking too loud and calling each other *bitch* and *bird* and *slag* a bit too often, and occasionally dancing with one another quite provocatively to the preband music.

The band took the stage and finished tuning their instruments. Bret leaned in to tell the women that he and "Aaron" were going to go talk with a few people they had met at a conference that he'd noticed were in the crowd, but they would love to buy a round of drinks in honor and celebration of the bride-to-be if they caught up with them later. Then he pulled "Aaron" away.

"So how'd the lobbyist ruse work with the chics you were talking to?" Bret asked.

"It didn't. To be honest, it didn't come up. I asked some generic questions, and then they never stopped talking—mostly to each other. They did invite me to do ecstasy with them later though."

"And you accepted, right?"

"I told them I'd think about it."

"What the fuck? Well, we have to make sure to meet back up with them now."

"Yes, sir."

Bret bought a round of beers, and then he and Carwyn headed off to scope out the place. The band had sort of an indie-dance-punk-synthpop sound. Carwyn was content to drink his beers and enjoy the music, but Bret was scouting the place to see if there was any better—or easier—"talent." It wasn't long before Bret suggested shots: "You need some liquid courage." He bought one shot for himself and two for Carwyn.

They tossed back their Jäger shots at the same time, and then Carwyn did his solo shot. When he pounded his shot glass down, he saw another round, as if by some sort of bar magic, already awaiting him. He and Bret lightly tapped their glasses and fired the shots back: tequila.

"You're an asshole."

"Me?" asked Bret, feigning complete innocence.

"You know tequila makes me black out."

"Sorry, Bro, I forgot."

"Bullshit you did. Whatever—one shot shouldn't do it anyway, but still."

Bret ordered another round of beers then said, "Now let's go mingle."

They walked around, checking out the people and the place. It was crowded, the band was good, and the drinks were only moderately overpriced. Bret and Carwyn each danced with a couple of different girls, the booze limbering their legs. When the band announced they would be taking a ten-minute break, Bret suggested more shots. Carwyn, as he always did after a few drinks, acquiesced to having a few more. Bret ordered some Dutch lemon gin, and Carwyn ordered another round of beers. He felt obligated to buy at least one round of drinks.

After they threw back their nasty gin shots, Bret suggested, "We should wait two or three songs after the band comes back on, and then we should try to find those British bitches." Carwyn didn't really like Bret's constant reference to women as *bitches*, but as he was definitely feeling a strong buzz, he paid little attention to his misogynistic friend.

Bret and Carwyn chilled in a less crowded area of the club for just one song before Bret got impatient and led the way around the place in an attempt to find his marks. They walked up to the upper level of the club to get a better view. From up there, the Brits were easy to spot. They were still wearing their devil horns. They were near the stage but also close to the bar, and they were dancing suggestively among themselves.

Bret led the way down. He walked up to one of the girls he had talked to earlier. Carwyn followed. One of the women Carwyn had talked to spotted him, and she pulled him into their group to dance. They tried to talk, but it was absolutely impossible to hear so close to the stage. Carwyn saw Bret making the universal let's-get-some-drinks gesture, tilting his head back slightly and drinking an imaginary beverage from an imaginary glass.

The women, who seemed like they would never turn down a free drink, definitely understood the sign language and followed Bret and Carwyn to the bar. Bret ordered ten shots of Black Haus, an eighty-proof German blackberry schnapps. It was a good selection. The girls all loved it, so Bret ordered one more round. After the second round, Bret approached one of the women and artlessly inquired as to the ecstasy offer that had been extended to Carwyn earlier. The reply he received caused him mixed feelings. The ladies had all popped their pills during the band's intermission, but "that stupid, off-her-face cow Sophie dropped the last of the pills down the toilet when she was taking hers."

Bret considered this development and figured that the good news was all the girls had taken the X and should be getting good and touchy-feely very soon. The bad news was that he didn't get to roll right along with them. Since he was not going to be able to partake in the ecstasy, Bret decided to make the leap and suggested that they all continue the party back at the girls' hotel. At least the woman he was talking to seemed to take to the idea. She shared the idea with the rest of her group, and they seemed game too. *Hallelujah*, Bret thought.

To ensure Carwyn's cooperation, Bret bought him another shot of tequila. This time Carwyn did not label Bret an asshole. Carwyn was already on his way, without ever really knowing it, to being blackout drunk. Bret and Carwyn rejoined the women on the dance floor, and after just a couple of songs with increasing levels of touching and rubbing, Bret suggested they head back to the hotel.

The girl who was currently rubbing on him agreed and informed him that they had a hotel on Kerkstraat just a few blocks away; further, they had three rooms. They could use the middle room, giving them a noise buffer zone so they would disturb fewer people. Bret was surprised by the level of logic exhibited by someone in such an altered state, but he alerted Carwyn to the development. A moment later they were all headed to the girls' hotel.

It was a quick walk to the hotel, but by the time they made it up to the room somehow only five of the eight women were still with them. Perhaps the other three had stayed at the club, made off with some other guys, or simply wandered off and got lost on the short walk.

Inside the hotel room, Bret was quick—lightning quick, really—to get one of the women out of her clothes. Then, standing on the bed, he goaded one of the women to her knees. Bret quickly let his pants fall to his ankles so that he could kick them across the room.

Carwyn was really in no shape to participate in any of the hedonistic activities even if he had wanted to. The last thing Carwyn remembered was all five of the Peterborough women in various states of undress and Bret bending one over the dresser drawer while making out with another.

16

DIRTY COPS WERE ONE of Aeneid's all time biggest pet peeves. She recognized the partial hypocrisy of her distaste for dirty cops, but the way Aeneid saw it, she and dirty cops were very different. Aeneid got rid of people that needed to be gotten rid of, and she was very good at it. She had killed approximately thirty people (she didn't really like to keep count). *But* she had certain principles, if not integrity.

Aeneid never caused a mark any undue pain or suffering. She never used primitive means to extract information from her targets (although there were others who would). Quite the opposite, actually: Aeneid made sure that certain information was contained. The dissimilarity that most distinguished Aeneid from the dirty cops that she abhorred was that she had never taken any oath to uphold the law. It was not her job to protect and serve, and she did not abuse power or responsibility for personal gain.

One of the things Aeneid hated about dirty cops was that she often had to clean up their messes. The dirty cop she had been following for the past few hours had dark eyes, a dark complexion, and reddish hair. He was some sort of genetic miracle—well, anomaly at least. *Miracle is stretching it*, she thought. Aeneid wasn't even sure the cop's features were real. Maybe he was a tanning salon junkie, or maybe he wore colored contacts, or maybe both. He surely would not have dyed his hair that color.

As Aeneid was following Lorenz, it hit her like a sucker punch. Despite certain dissimilarities, she wasn't all that different from the type of cops she so vehemently despised. In fact, she was worse. She presented multiple faces to the world—too many faces. She barely even knew what face was hers anymore. Recently, there had been far too many times when she had looked at herself in the mirror and didn't really recognize the woman starring back at her. And that terrified the hell out of her.

Her self-reflective fear had almost prompted her to dispose of Officer Lorenz along with the other greedy, stupid cops who had made the latest mess she was now required to clean up. But her murderous impulse was selfish and self-protective. By getting rid of Lorenz and his crew, she would be getting rid of a constant reminder of her own flaws and failings. She would, in a way, be shattering a mirror that reflected the worst of herself back to her. She wondered why the *gentilhuomini* had decided to associate with Lorenz in the first place.

As much as she wanted to rid the world of Lorenz and his crew (and rid herself of the cognitive dissonance), Aeneid would ignore Lorenz, Kerrigan, Murphy, and Rossi, at least for the time being. She would stick to her assignment. Her assignment would be easy—too easy—but it may very well turn out to be the worst decision of her life. She knew that once she compromised her integrity and principles, she would never be the same again.

— 17 —

When Carwyn first woke up, miraculously only slightly hung-over, he had absolutely no clue where he was. Then, as a few scattered pieces of the night slowly began to come back to him, he looked over and saw a woman he didn't recognize lying next to him on a bed that he knew was not his. She was stark naked except for a faux wedding veil. Seeing the veil jogged Carwyn's memory, and in an instant most of the night—up to seeing the women from Peterborough stripping out of their clothes—came rushing back to him. But he couldn't remember everything.

To make matters worse, the woman lying next to him in that veil could only mean one thing. As awareness rippled through his mind, he simultaneously felt nervous, anxious, embarrassed, jaded, ashamed, guilty, disturbed. As the rush of recollection and emotion hit him, he reacted, almost as if by reflex, by springing from the bed in an attempt to distance himself from the affianced Brit in the bed.

His attempted escape was clumsy, and he fell from the bed, cracking his head against the wall on his way to the floor. He remained flat on the floor, basking in his shame.

At the sound of Carwyn's failed getaway, a woman emerged from the bathroom. She walked over to where Carwyn was picking himself up off the floor and noticed the ashen look on his face. Putting two and two together, she laughed and then reassured him, "No need to bite your arm off trying to get out of here. Jackie there's not the bride-to-be, just the last one to wear the veil. We took turns wearing it throughout the course of the night so we could all get a share of the attention. A hen party is a bit of a John Thomas magnet. Anyway, Layla, the real bride-to-be, is safe and sound in her own room. I imagine your friend is still next door where the one-man mini-orgy took place last night. You just zonked out, and then you somehow ended up in here with the two of us."

Carwyn was relieved but still felt rather awkward and embarrassed. "Um, thanks for enlightening me," he said, rubbing his head. "I was actually really worried about that ... in case you hadn't noticed. Who's John Thomas?" With another laugh, the Brit informed him that is was just slang for pecker.

"Oh. Well, I guess I should gather my friend. Do you know what time it is?"

"Half past ten."

"Thanks, and thanks again for reassuring me that I didn't sleep with the bride-to-be. Should I just go next door and knock?"

"Sure."

"Well, um, enjoy the rest of your trip."

"Thanks, and it's good to know there are still a few decent blokes left in this world."

Carwyn went next door and knocked. No answer. He waited a few seconds then knocked louder. He could hear movement. A woman came to the door in nothing but a T-shirt. It was just long enough. The woman at the door looked a little confused. Carwyn quickly scanned the room to see four passed out naked Peterboroughians

Bret was not in the room. Carwyn quickly craned his neck to peer into the bathroom. Not in there either. The girl at the door hadn't said anything and was still staring blankly from the threshold. Finally she managed a word: "Yes?"

Satisfied that Bret wasn't in the room, Carwyn offered his reply. "Sorry. Wrong room." Blushing, he summarily headed for the nearest exit.

Outside, the late-morning sun only hurt Carwyn's eyes for a moment; then, after his eyes adjusted, it became a source of welcome warmth. Carwyn's solitary walk back to the hotel was rather pleasant. As he neared the red light district, although the adult stores, sex shows, and renowned windows were all still there, it seemed like a different place than it had been the night before. It was almost as if someone had splashed rubbing alcohol over the entire area and wiped away the gaudy, red-tinted stage make-up to reveal bridges, canals, architecture, flowers, and churches. *What a paradoxical city*, he thought.

When he got to the hotel room door, Carwyn pulled his wallet from his back pocket to retrieve his room key. He inserted his key and entered the room. Bret was sprawled face-first on the bed. Carwyn picked up a pillow and whacked the ever-loving shit out of Bret a couple times. He turned over slowly, gruffly, indignantly, only to get struck right across the face with multiple pillow strikes.

Bret mechanically raised his middle finger in Carwyn's direction and hoarsely grumbled, "What the fuck are you doing?" He didn't even seem all that phased by the pillow barrage.

"You got me drunk, encouraged me to take multiple tequila shots, let me pass out in a hotel room full of promiscuous English women—which, I guess, sounds like an absolutely insane thing to complain about—but anyway. Meanwhile, you were doing God knows what. Then, to top it all off, you ditched me, so when I woke up this morning and finally figured out where the hell I was, I felt like shit because I thought I had slept with an engaged woman!"

"Did you?"

"No, I just said that I *thought* I did."

"Why the hell not, bro?"

"Well, I guess the ultimate reason is that I passed out, thanks mostly to you. But, well, there is also the fact that oh, I dunno, that would have been a damn shitty thing to do—she's engaged to be married."

"She wasn't married last night, was she? How you feeling, by the way? Despite your attacking me like some PMS-ing sorority girl, I feel fine. A little tired, but that's about it."

"Whether she was married yet or not is beside the point. And I feel fine, more or less."

"Dude, you shoulda hit that. I mean, I had like four or five of those sluts on my junk."

"You have a sickness. That must be it—a certifiable sickness. How would you feel if a group of four or five foreign dudes ran the train on Rebecca?"

"Shut up, fuck stick."

"Oh, a double standard, is it?"

Bret sat up and punched Carwyn on the arm.

Typical. "Yep, definitely a double standard. You can be a cheating douchebag, but Rebecca … don't even *talk* about her. Anyway, get your pathetic man-whore ass into the shower. We have shit to do today, and I'm not going to let the fact that you're a philandering sexaholic get in the way."

Carwyn was more or less numb to Bret's actions at this point. He knew that Bret had made the rounds back in his single days, but he had had no idea that Bret had little or no respect for the sanctity of a monogamous relationship or women in general. *Funny how friendship can lead you to overlook some pretty despicable stuff.*

Bret rolled off the bed and plodded to the shower. When he was out, Carwyn hopped in. The first stop of the day was a coffee shop—a real one—to power up, not down. While drinking their coffee, they discussed their itinerary for the day: the Van Gogh Museum, the Rijksmuseum, the Heineken Brewery Experience. Bret suggested they make another coffee shop stop before the Van Gogh Museum. Carwyn assented, even though this time they wouldn't be drinking coffee.

Not having any specific plans for after the museums and the brewery, and since Bret needed to do some light reading (which meant take a shit), they decided to stop back by the hotel. Carwyn was totally unaware of what awaited him there.

Upon entering their room, Carwyn and Bret both noticed that something didn't seem quite right. They had left the do-not-disturb sign on the door, but both beds had the comforters pulled up. A few items looked like they had been moved. One of the room lights was on, and the bathroom door was shut with the light on. Bret and Carwyn noticed the changes, but they were more confused than nervous or scared. They had no reason to suspect any danger.

Bret pointed to the closed bathroom door, motioning that he was going to inspect the room. Still unsuspecting, he made light of the situation with a mock covert hand signal, as if he was a Navy SEAL or some covert operative on a secret mission. He opened the door and tip-toed into the bathroom.

Carwyn stood behind Bret. The shower curtain was closed. Just as Bret approached the shower, the curtain was yanked back from the inside, catching Bret and Carwyn completely off guard.

— 18 —

THE WELL-DRESSED BUSINESSMAN'S HIGHLY anticipated deal closing had not gone the way he had hoped—the way he had thought it would. Deals sometimes fell through. That was the nature of any business. This had been one of those deals. No insignificant amount of time had gone into all the preparations for the deal that had just fallen through. The wasted time, effort, and money annoyed the man but not much more than if he had been caught in the rain without an umbrella or spilled brown mustard on a nice tie.

This was not the first time a deal had fallen through. Hell, it probably wouldn't be the last. The businessman would simply start working on another deal—maybe even this very day. The businessman found that it was sometimes more fun when a deal didn't get done. The men he hired on a temporary basis to help him conduct his transactions and deals certainly got to have a little more fun.

Although the businessman had successfully brokered a large number of similar deals and turned quite the handsome profit, there had been two—now three—deals that had never been fully concluded. The reason for two out of the three failures had been incomplete research. However, there had been one escape. The escapee had not lived to see her next birthday.

— 19 —

STARTLED BY THE PERSON behind the curtain, Bret jumped back, banged into the sink, and almost flipped over it. Carwyn, unsure of what to do, just yelled out. Well, it wasn't much of a yell really. It certainly wouldn't have gotten anybody's attention. Their pulses quickened as their reflexive fight-or-flight responses kicked in. However, any fear or perception of a threat dissipated just about as quickly as it had been triggered. As the intruder stepped from behind the curtain, she was instantly recognizable, "Rebecca?" God only knew what emotion or emotions replaced Bret's fear.

Carwyn's fear was replaced by severe annoyance. *There goes the rest of our trip*, he thought.

Rebecca was cracking up but managed to say, "None other. I got you guys good. You should have seen your faces!" As her laughter subsided and Bret and Carwyn's shock wore off, Carwyn asked, "How the hell did you end up in here?"

"Oh, I have my ways," she said, pretending to be mysterious, and let it hang in the air for just a second before she elaborated. "Seriously, though, I knew you guys were staying at this hotel through my last convo with Bret, and when I arrived this afternoon, I made my way straight here. I just told the person at the desk that I was Mrs. Hightower. I was washing my face when I heard you guys coming in, so I decided to give you a little scare. You really should have seen your faces. Bret's in particular was priceless. You would have thought I was the grim reaper or something."

"You're lucky he didn't shit himself. That's what we came back to the room for—for Bret to shit."

Ignoring Carwyn's comment, Bret asked, "Hun, what *are* you doing here? I mean, this is craziness. I thought you were gonna be researching and writing and working this whole time."

"Yeah, I was, but I got some things done early, had some free time, and decided to surprise you. Isn't this great!"

"Well, it's a surprise all right," interjected Carwyn. He was thinking, *No, it definitely is not great.*

"Well, Bret's all mine now, Carwyn, so your silly boy time is over. I've got the vagina, you don't. Sorry, Car."

"It's not like he needs yours," Carwyn *wanted* to say. But Bret was his best friend, and if there was ever some fiery fallout from Bret's infidelities, Carwyn didn't want to be in the middle of it. What Carwyn actually said, unable to contain his frustration over the new development, was, "I knew I smelled something."

Now it was Rebecca's turn to ignore Carwyn. "So, babe," she said to Bret, "this is going to be wonderful. I'm so excited. I have a hotel booked for tonight close to the airport. Then we have a flight tomorrow to Paris, where I have the most amazing room booked for two nights. We have a view overlooking the Seine. Then I have us booked for a night in Monte-Carlo, because I know how much you love casinos, and finally, I got us a great room in an adorable little place in Venice for two nights. It's going to be so romantic. I can't wait!" By this time Rebecca's voice was actually starting to anger Carwyn.

Rebecca suggested that she and Bret take their luggage to the new hotel right away but that the three of them should have dinner together. To be civil, Carwyn agreed to join them for dinner (at a place Rebecca had already picked out, of course). In reality, he was pissed. *What the hell am I supposed to do now?* He didn't really hate Rebecca (he very rarely hated anybody), but he sure disliked the shit out of her right about now.

Bret turned on the TV before he went into the bathroom. He wanted some sort of noise so he didn't feel like he had an audience for his light reading (i.e., his heavy and probably hemp-scented shit). Rebecca and Carwyn sat down on separate beds. Neither was interested in the television, and neither was going to be a big conversationalist at that moment.

The silence was broken by the sound of the toilet flushing followed by the sound of running water from the sink. Then another flush. When Bret emerged from the bathroom, Carwyn couldn't resist making Bret sweat by saying, "I was just about to tell your lovely fiancée about Sophie. Man, was she hot or what?"

Without so much as a fraction of a second of hesitation, Bret skirted the question. "She definitely seemed like your type."

Expertly done, thought Carwyn.

Rebecca said to Bret, "Okay, well, I'm going to arrange for a cab to pick us up and take us to our new hotel." To Carwyn, she said, "Dinner is at eight." Then she picked up the phone and did her arranging. Rebecca told Carwyn about the restaurant and how to get there if he chose to walk. A couple minutes later, Bret and Rebecca made their way down to the lobby to wait for the cab. As they left, Bret simply said to Carwyn, "See you at dinner." *How could someone so lascivious and philandering also be so servile? Maybe it's the money. Maybe it's some postmodern, poisoned type of love. Maybe it's a form of penance. Maybe it's just the only way Bret can rationalize or reconcile his reprehensible behavior.*

20

SINCE CARWYN HAD DECIDED not to walk to the restaurant, he was actually a little early. The place didn't look like much from the outside, but once inside Carwyn could tell that Rebecca had either done her homework or gotten lucky. He spoke with the maître d' and was shown to the table. He ordered a beer and waited for Bret and Rebecca to arrive. They showed up about fifteen minutes late, and Bret apologized by saying, "Sorry, Bec and I hadn't seen each other for a while, so it took a little longer than we thought to get ready, if you know what I mean."

With compounded annoyance Carwyn retorted, "Well, you should be good and ready by now." Bret didn't seem to realize that Carwyn was alluding to the threesome and reverse gang-bang that Bret had so recently taken part in. It made Carwyn feel better anyway.

Carwyn's annoyance aside, the food and the service confirmed what Carwyn had gleaned from his initial impression of the décor of the restaurant.

When the bill came, Rebecca picked it up and provided a credit card as payment to the server. She told Carwyn, "Treating you to a nice dinner is the least I can do for bringing your extended man date to an abrupt end. But just think: you can go window shopping tonight and pick out something really nice for yourself." Carwyn chose not to respond.

After signing the credit card slip, Rebecca stood up, and Bret followed suit. Carwyn was the last to stand. They walked out together, but they were headed in different directions, both literally and figuratively.

"Car," Bret said, "I've had a blast, man. Sorry I'm ditching you, bro, but one day you're going to find a girl—probably in Russia—who'll force you to alter your plans too. Oh, and if you have any extra time on your hands throughout the rest of your trip, I expect you to use it to work on a kick-ass best man speech."

"I'll see what I can do. But there's going to be so much dirt I'll have to edit out, I don't know how much material I'll have left to work with."

"Funny."

"Well, see you back in Boston." And with that, the two shook hands and went their separate ways.

After the dinner and the good-byes, it was about ten o'clock, and Carwyn decided to walk. He probably had about a thirty-minute walk ahead of him. As he had absolutely no plans whatsoever, he didn't mind. When he got back to the heart of the red light district, it had come alive in all its commercially seedy glory. At first Carwyn tried not to look. When that proved unsuccessful, he tried not to look directly or noticeably at the women in their windows; but the scantily clad women dancing, writhing, or unabashedly beckoning men or women or both to step inside their offices were not easy to ignore.

He couldn't help but think about what Rebecca had said. He came to the conclusion that being uncommitted and all alone in this city with no real timetable, deadline, or agenda, there was no conclusive reason not to at least take a closer look.

Instead of doing so, Carwyn first went back to his hotel on the outskirts of the red light district. In his room, he used the restroom, brushed his teeth, gargled with mouthwash, and then washed his face. As he dried his face, he took a good look at himself in the mirror. He had to laugh. Was he really freshening up for an unknown, unnamed prostitute whom he had not even definitively decided he would visit? *I guess I am*, he thought to himself as he took off his shirt, applied yet another layer of deodorant, and then changed.

Outside, the sky was crystal clear. It was a beautiful, crisp night, and the temperature hovered at right about perfect degrees Celsius. As he walked through the brisk night air and quickly emerged back into the heart of the red light district, he thought about the unique city he was ambling through. He had already concluded that it was one of the most paradoxical cities in the world.

It was an absolutely beautiful city with winding canals, unique architecture, a rainbow of tulips and other flowers, and some of the best museums in the world. It just also happened to be a hippie mecca where one could legally purchase more than one type of drug (some stores even provided ratings on the different types of high you could get from the various mushrooms you could buy). And of course there was the prostitution. Sure, plenty of other cities in the world had legalized prostitution. Sure, there were cities in the United States where prostitution was legal. Sure, the entire country of New Zealand had legalized prostitution. But this was the *crème de la crème* of purchasable affections.

Carwyn circled the environs and alleyways of the red light district for more than an hour. He took it all in, trying to determine if he was actually going to go through with it. He was looking for the perfect woman, probably just as much to delay and discourage himself from going through with what he was contemplating as to make going through with it worthwhile.

He'd seen her once in his multiple laps through the alleys and past those one-of-a-kind windows, but it was more of an unconscious perception than a full observation and appreciation. As he continued, he saw scattered windows with two women. He even made a pass down what seemed to be fetish row, where all the fat and old women were located. Carwyn had even seen that segregation was alive and well in the oldest profession in the world: all the black women were in the same row just on the edge of the district.

The number of men and even women and children walking around the area sightseeing and window shopping was unbelievable. This made Carwyn all the more uncomfortable. People would actually see him go in and, what was worse, see him come out. Still Carwyn strolled. There wasn't too much else to do anyway. Then, in the narrowest of alleys, he saw her again.

This time he really saw her, took her all in. She was clad in black and pink lingerie—a sort of teddy or corset, opaque thigh-high stockings, and a matching thong. She was the classiest looking of all the women he had seen. When Carwyn thought that to himself, he almost laughed out loud. But the woman in the window was absolutely gorgeous.

She was unsettlingly cute-innocent-sexy. Carwyn hesitated just a moment then went up to her window. He caught a quick glimpse of his own reflection in the window and thought for a fleeting instant that he might turn and walk briskly away. He didn't. And that is just how close our lives can come to unfolding completely differently.

Part 2

(HOW BEFORE CAN ALTER AND
PERMEATE NOW AND AFTER)

— 21 —

AN ENIGMATICALLY ATTRACTIVE WOMAN opened her door, and Carwyn walked inside. She quoted a price, which Carwyn agreed to with a shy nod, and then she led him down a narrow hallway. She stuck out her hand for the money. It was definitely an awkward situation, at least for Carwyn. It was unlikely the woman from the window felt the same weight in the air. Once Carwyn handed over the money, however, the awkward air seemed to float away, and all the weight that Carwyn had perceived was gone.

"Where are you from?"

"Canada," he lied, without being exactly sure why.

"Oh really? Me too. What part?"

Shit. Busted, he thought. "Are you really from Canada?" he asked.

"Yep. Ottawa. My mom was Canadian, my dad American."

Was she being truthful? There was no way to tell. "Well, damn. I have to admit I lied. I'm from the United States, actually. How did you end up in Amsterdam?"

"It's a long story. The short version is that I came to study abroad in Europe, and I never left."

"How old are you," Carwyn asked.

"Twenty-six. You?"

"Twenty-eight."

"Well, you going to take off your clothes?"

To Carwyn, the question seemed to come out of nowhere, but presumably she did have to keep the flow of customers moving.

"Uh, sure."

He began to take off his clothes, and the awkwardness came back for a moment. She grabbed a condom from a basket, directed him toward the bed. Then she took him into her mouth. Any nerves had subsided, and he was instantly fully hard. She opened the condom and slowly unrolled it onto him with her mouth. She fell purposefully to her back and pulled him toward her gently. She grabbed him and guided him directly to the opening waiting between her legs. He slid in, not overly easily but without any real effort. *Ah ...*

Once he was inside her, all semblance of uneasiness was gone. Nature took over. It was like a roller coaster with no bumps or head jerks. Smooth. Good, fun, natural, scintillating. Quick. Before he knew it, and definitely before he really wanted it to be, it was over. And then the awkwardness briefly returned. Condom off. Condom tied in a knot. Condom in the trash.

Without even being consciously aware of it, Carwyn dressed again. And then they just talked—for only a minute or two, but it was easy, natural.

And in that random instant, as absolutely improbable and impractical as it was, Carwyn felt as if he had never been more at ease in his life, which of course was extremely weird verging on absurd. He was, after all, engaging in postcoital idle but friendly chitchat with a professional sex worker. But then, of course, he had to leave.

"Thank you," she said in a cute yet businesslike (and therefore mildly disappointing) way.

"Um, yeah, thank you." And with that he began the exodus down the steps and out the door. Carwyn tried to act as nonchalant as possible.

As soon as the red-lit door closed (and was almost immediately reopened by another customer), he felt empty. But this was a different kind of emptiness—completely different. It was not an I-just-got-drunk-and-had-meaningless-sex-with-some-random-fashion-design-major kind of emptiness but a novel and surprising variety of emptiness. He had just experienced what seemed like a near perfect intimate encounter—which, Carwyn thought, *is pretty messed up, considering it was with a prostitute*—and he wished he could feel exactly the same way on a regular basis. *Odd*, Carwyn thought, and in the next instant he thought, *Tomorrow!*

Then and there, Carwyn decided he would go back to the same window at the same time tomorrow to ask—*Shit, I didn't even get her name*—to dinner. With his mind made up, he made his way back to his hotel room. He sure hadn't seen the twists of this day coming, even though it had started with him falling out of a stranger's bed.

22

THE WAY JOHNNY SAW it, Lorenz and his crew were starting to be more trouble than they were worth. One problem was that because they were being paid by the association, they thought they were a real part of the association. On top of that, they were greedy—and they were too ambitious. However, regardless of their ambition and greed, they were quite lazy. They were also impatient and careless. They were careless because they assumed that their badges and their association with the *gentiluomini privati* placed them above the law and shielded them from all scrutiny.

Not only did they assume they were above the law, but they also assumed they were indispensable, untouchable. Although they were neither indispensible nor untouchable, they couldn't just be put on ice without drawing too much unwanted heat.

The recent fuckup wasn't really all Lorenz and his fucking goof troop's fault anyway. It was just bad timing. Shit timing. But Lorenz starting to act like he was a capo—that kinda shit just wasn't gonna fly. Maybe if they just knocked off Lorenz the other three elbows would remember their place. And killing one cop would be easier to get away with. On the other hand, without Lorenz in charge, the other three might just fuck up more, or they might be scared straight and try to turn their backs on the *gentiluomini*. A war was something nobody wanted.

Well, in they end, the association with Lorenz and his wannabes was just like any marriage: it had its ups and its downs, its benefits and its negative consequences. For now the *gentiluomini privati* could just let it ride, but perhaps a divorce was immanent.

— 23 —

THE MORNING AFTER CARWYN's first-ever prostitute liaison, he checked out of his hotel and into a much cheaper hostel. Then he was out of ideas. Because it was quick and easy, and especially because it was cheap, he had lunch—despite his better judgment—at FEBO again. *Now what?* he thought. There was surely plenty to do, but he didn't know where or when to do it. With no ideas and not yet having succumbed to the smartphone craze, Carwyn went to an internet café to search for something to do. He decided on the Diamond Museum and the Vodka Museum.

After the museums, he picked a place where he could sit outside to eat dinner. He was playing the scene of asking a prostitute out to dinner over and over in his head. The idea seemed to grow more idiotic the more he thought about it. *How desperate could a guy be?* he thought.

He ordered a cheap meal, ate quickly, and drank four beers with his dinner. Carwyn's alcohol tolerance seemed to fluctuate greatly, and after he had paid for his dinner and drinks, he noticed that he had a buzz. It was enough to take the edge off, and Carwyn stood from his table with renewed verve and purpose—even if his purpose was to ask a prostitute out on a date.

Carwyn proceeded to walk to where he had been last night. He didn't see the woman he was looking for in the window. *Shit!* He continued walking, and when he strode past her window a second time, she was there. *Yes!* Her presence in the window was only advantageous if Carwyn could act on it, which, it turned out, he was unable to do. He chickened out, picked up his pace, and walked right past. *I am an idiot.*

Carwyn walked to the middle of a dimly lit bridge and stood gazing into the canal that flowed beneath his feet. As he gazed down at the distorted, gently rippling reflection of his face in the murky canal water below, he thought about what he was doing. His reflection, which looked almost as if it was trapped in the canal, rendered him philosophical. *Every action we take changes us. It might not be profound. It might not even be noticeable. But every day we wake up a different person from the one we were the day before, and we change countless times throughout the course of any single day.*

The water flowing beneath Carwyn's feet was ever changing, flowing from old sources toward uncertain destinations; the reflected image of Carwyn's face was constantly, subtly changing; and Carwyn was different in imperceptible ways merely because he had come to stand on the bridge in the first place.

Amid his reflection and contemplation, Carwyn noticed a lone smooth rock by his foot. He wondered how it had gotten there, all by itself. After gazing at his reflection a moment longer, Carwyn bent down and picked up the rock. He tossed it from his right hand to his left and back to his right again. Then he dropped it into the flowing canal waters below, into the very spot where his reflection had been rippling constantly and subtly changing for upward of ten minutes now. When the rock hit the water, it made a plunking sound and completely altered Carwyn's reflection.

In the very instant after he dropped the smooth rock into the center of his reflection below, Carwyn turned and walked away from the bridge. That rock had fundamentally changed the liquid version of Carwyn's face that had been starring back up to him from out of the murky water. If Carwyn had stayed put on the bridge, then the miniature waves created by the smooth rock would have subsided, and Carwyn's face would have settled back to its previous state.

By leaving the bridge when he did, a mere second or two after releasing the rock, Carwyn had permanently altered his reflection. Now he needed a rock to drop into his real life, to fundamentally change him—not just his reflection. He resolved to go back again to the smooth glass window from the night before.

But when he did go back, the woman from the night before was gone again. *Damn it!* He continued walking past the window and out of the narrow alley. As he passed the window, he caught a fleeting glimpse of his reflection. He somehow looked different. *Surely*, he thought, *it's all in my head ... but isn't that where the most meaningful changes originate?*

He wandered around for more than an hour and then made his

way back to the window for the fourth time that night. He felt about as stupid as he thought it was possible to feel. Still, as he approached the portentous window, he already had a fifty-euro note and a twenty-euro note in his hand. The notes were folded up small so that with his hand clenched, no one could see them. He walked right up, and she opened her door. He handed her the money before a word was spoken, and she led him back to her room.

"You were here last night."

Carwyn, embarrassed, made no reply, but at least she remembered him. *That's gotta mean something!*

"Well, get out of your clothes."

"Go to dinner with me," he practically exclaimed.

"What?"

Carwyn felt more than a little silly, but he continued, "Um, I didn't come here to have sex with you. I came to pay you for your time now so that I could ask you to dinner with me tomorrow night." Even just the fraction of a second of silence that knifed through the small, square room was too much for Carwyn, so he added anxiously, "As bizarre as that might sound."

The woman standing in front of him was cutely, innocently, even angelically beautiful, yet her chosen line of work was far from innocent. That juxtaposition made her, in Carwyn's eyes, the most intriguing and physically appealing person he had ever seen. He was besotted.

After an additional pause, the woman responded, "Well, that is a new one to me. I've had men offer to pay me to do them with a strap-on, to pee on them, to let them pee on me, and—well, a number of other completely off-the-wall requests. I even had one guy ask me to punch him in the face while we were doing it. I negotiated down to just a hard slap. He paid me two hundred and fifty euros extra for just a couple of slaps. But no one has ever asked me out on a date. I must say, it's kind of flattering ..."

Flattering? Carwyn was bordering on humiliated.

"... but I can't have dinner with you tomorrow night. I'm working ..."

Embarrassment exacerbated by the sting of rejection.

"... I can do lunch though."

Lunch. Shit! Wait. Holy shit! Carwyn, agog and heart racing, attempted a jubilation-hiding joke. "Well, I'd like a discount then."

Luckily for Carwyn, the woman seemed to get his joke, but there was going to be no discount.

"Sorry, all sales final, but if you can be here at three in the morning, that's when I finish my shift.

You can come with me to get some late-night food, and that would be like two for the price of one."

"Deal."

As Carwyn started to leave, the woman from the window gave him an inquisitive look. "Don't you want to know my name?"

"Oh. Well, yes, of course I do. I'm Carwyn, by the way."

"Carwyn. That's what? Irish or Welsh, right? Well, it's nice to meet you Carwyn. I'm Vivian.

Feeling quite foolish and exceptionally proud of himself at the same time, Carwyn left and headed directly back to the hostel. He was in a dorm-style room with twelve beds. He switched his cell phone alarm to vibrate and set it for 2:20 in the morning. He put his phone in his pocket so that the vibrations would definitely wake him. That would give him enough time to wake himself up, make himself presentable, and get to that wonderful window with the best view money could buy a little before three.

When vibrations in his pants woke Carwyn up in a dark hostel dorm room at twenty minutes past two in the morning, he was so startled and disoriented that he damn near fell out of his top bunk. Once out of the bunk with his feet planted firmly and safely on the ground, he felt perfectly awake. He grabbed what he needed from his backpack and got ready in the dark. When he got outside, he had about twenty minutes to kill. Carwyn sat down on a random bench and looked out into the night.

Carwyn was stationed outside Vivian's window several minutes before three. A couple minutes later, Vivian came around a corner in jeans and an orange-hooded Ajax sweatshirt.

"Three, huh?"

"Well, some girls work more or less all night, but I actually finished at two. I wanted to go home, shower, and change. Although I didn't think you would actually show up."

"Well, here I am. And I'm very pleased to know that you showered and changed all just for me. So where to?"

"McDonald's. I didn't have dinner before my shift, and I'm starving. Sorry, I know McDonald's isn't very exciting."

"Exciting is overrated."

Vivian led the way to a twenty-four-hour McDonald's a few blocks away. In passable Dutch, she ordered a *groenteburger*, a small order of fries, and a Fanta. In English, Carwyn ordered a medium order of fries and a small coffee. When they got their orders, Vivian led them upstairs to a table by a window.

"What is that thing?" Carwyn asked, referring to her burger.

"It's a vegetable croquet burger."

"Are you a vegetarian?"

"No, I'm just as much of a carnivore as the next girl. This unappetizing-looking sandwich is just surprisingly good."

"Good. I don't want to have thrown away my money."

"You are awfully jocular for someone who recently made the type of transaction you did … I mean, that is a bit weird and desperate, isn't it?"

"Jocular? Nice—not a word you hear used very often in conversation. But, well, I pride myself on my jocularity, and I guess I tend to make jokes when I'm nervous. Besides, if I'm weird and desperate, what does that make you?"

Without missing a beat, Vivian responded, "Charitable."

"Touché. So are you gonna tell me how you ended up in your line of work?" Carwyn had immediate second thoughts about asking such a personal question, but he couldn't very well un-ask it.

"I might tell you," Vivian said, "but certainly not in McDonald's … and I pride myself on my vocabulary, thank you very much. I was an English major, after all. Why would you be nervous?"

"I was an English major too. As for being nervous, you yourself said I was weird and desperate. I suppose that's reason enough to be a bit nervous."

"I suppose, and congratulations on a pointless degree."

"Well, gee, thanks, but I actually just got my masters in journalism."

"And, what, you're here in Amsterdam to sow some wild oats before settling down with a big-boy job?"

"Actually, I came here with my best friend from high school for a sort of postgraduation bachelor getaway."

There was a momentary silence that seemed to reveal what Vivian was thinking before she spoke. "Please don't tell me that you're engaged after what you've pulled the past couple nights."

"I'm not. My friend Bret is engaged, but what he's done over the course of this trip is worse than my being here with you now and last night combined. Anyway, his fiancée randomly showed up, and they're off in Paris now."

"Worse than being with me? What is that supposed to mean?"

"I just mean worse than it would be if I were actually the engaged one." Carwyn then proceeded to recount most of his and Bret's trip up to Rebecca's arrival. He didn't mention the part about Karolina, and he actually felt a little bit guilty about it.

"Wow," said Vivian. "No offense, but I think it's guys like your friend Bret who led me to where I am now. But that's a story I can tell you in the privacy of my tiny little apartment, if you still want to hear it."

"I'll listen to any story you have to tell." Immediately after his response, Carwyn felt that he had come on way too strong, or too cheesy, or just too lame. This girl definitely had him second guessing himself. Vivian didn't seem to notice, however; or if she noticed, she didn't seem to mind. Anyway, Vivian's smile eclipsed any self-doubt Carwyn may have had.

Vivian and Carwyn sorted their trash into separate containers to be recycled and headed downstairs and out to the street. It was quite cool, and a crisp breeze made it feel almost cold. Vivian nuzzled into Carwyn's body for a little extra warmth. Carwyn liked that. A lot. They walked about fifteen minutes before they came to Vivian's building. She led the way up to her unit. Her apartment was small—a studio—and sparsely decorated. There was a laptop on a small desk but no TV. There was one room that doubled as a bedroom and a living room, a surprisingly nice bathroom, and a small kitchen area.

"I told you it was small."

"It's plenty big enough for you and one honored guest."

"So what are you going to do when he shows up?"

Carwyn was really digging this girl. She took the definite weirdness of the current situation in stride, she didn't allow any awkwardness to fester, and she took his playful jabs for what they were: schoolboy flirting. On top of taking his jabs and quips and putting up with some nerve-induced bad jokes, she returned a few punches of her own.

"Ouch," Carwyn said, feigning indignation. "How long have you lived in this shoebox?"

"Well, I had to move into the box when I lost my soul."

Wow, that was corny, Carwyn thought, *but in a good way, I guess.* "Um, and how long ago was that?"

"About five months."

Carwyn sat down on Vivian's futon.

"Did I say you were allowed on my bed?"

"Um ..." Carwyn didn't really know what to say, but Vivian saved him.

"Kidding. Relax. Make yourself comfortable." Vivian was surprised by how comfortable she felt around Carwyn and with him in her apartment.

"Thanks," Carwyn responded, and he made himself comfortable. "This is my listening posture," he said. "I believe you have a story to tell."

"So, do you really want to hear about how I ended up as a young woman working in the world's oldest profession?"

"Yes. I really do."

"Okay, well"—she sat down beside him on her futon—"once upon a time in a land far, far away called Canada, I was born, and then I graduated high school, and after that I went to college, where I majored in English. In the beginning of the second semester of my junior year, I met this guy, also a junior, who I thought was Prince Charming—you know, blah, blah, blah, silly girl feelings and all that stuff. Anyway, we began quote unquote officially dating in my senior year. Things were good. I came to assume that he and I would move in somewhere together after we graduated, but—to shorten this part of the story—he was secretly both an evil pig and far too fond of cocaine." Here Vivian paused for the first of multiple times in her story before gathering the strength to continue describing what was obviously a painful set of experiences. "He—my boyfriend at the time, Rob—slept with my mom and cheated on me with three or four or more other girls too. In my mom's defense, I honestly think he might have actually drugged her. I'm telling you, this guy was an epic cretin. And that is all I'll say about that part of the story for now. But needless to say, my dream of happily ever after was not going to be coming true any time soon."

Carwyn thought about interjecting by saying something to the effect of, "That is fucked up," but instead he just listened intently and let Vivian tell her story. He sensed that despite the fact that it brought certain painful memories to the surface, she needed to tell it.

"For some reason at some point after I called it quits with Rob, I decided to apply to law school. And before I go any further, I know what you're probably thinking: she has got to be making this stuff up. Believe me, I wish I was, but unfortunately I'm not. So anyway, in law school I joined a public interest group, and I quickly became interested in international law and human rights. When I found out about a semester abroad at the University of Amsterdam that was also affiliated with The Hague, I jumped at the opportunity. Okay, so I'm just gonna shorten the story again here. I met an older man that worked for the ICJ, the International Court of Justice. I was starstruck, I guess you could say, so I allowed his flirtations and ignored minor indiscretions. But then he crossed the line, and I let him know it. He was married— with three kids, I believe it was. I guess he didn't take kindly to my rebuke of his continued advances. He said some very disgusting and damaging things about me, and since it was my word against his, all the lies he told resulted in my dismissal from the program. Mind you, this was after—and you're only the second person I have ever told this to, but I feel like it's okay to tell you, and maybe I just need to share it—after he summoned me to his office and tried to force himself on me. I trusted him. I respected him, and he tried to—to force himself on me. So, as one hundred percent absolutely absurd as it sounds, and as crazy it is, I took control of my life and my body in the one way I thought I could, and I ended up here in this shoebox apartment working out of a window."

Carwyn wasn't sure how to respond. He felt angry and uncomfortable and sad all at the same time, but he also felt a spark of a connection and a unique closeness with Vivian. Her vulnerability made him want to comfort and protect her, but her inner strength and courage made him respect and admire her and yearn to learn more about her, to *experience* more of her.

Recognizing Carwyn's uneasiness, Vivian added with a smile, "But here seems pretty good right about now."

After a brief silence during which Vivian and Carwyn sat looking at each other, Carwyn inquired, "You really have kinda lost your soul, haven't you?" He hoped it didn't come out sounding cheap or forced or like he was making a joke or otherwise making light of her story. She could see the sincerity in his eyes.

"Yeah, I guess I have," she said, and to attempt to lighten the mood and continue the allegory of the old running shoe, she concluded, "and with no sole and nowhere to run, I decided to move into the shoebox."

There was another brief period of silence. It never seemed awkward. The instant feeling of comfort between Vivian and Carwyn was beautifully and perplexingly calming, invigorating, and refreshing all at the same time.

"I think that you are stronger but also more vulnerable than you realize and more remarkable than you give yourself credit for."

"Do you mean that?" Vivian's tone seemed to be more hopeful than curious.

"Yes."

"Thank you. And I mean that. And thank you for listening to me. I guess I've never really told all of that to anyone. I think I needed to share that whole story, and I don't think I could have had a better listener. But enough about me. Tell me something about you, something you have never told anyone. What kind of skeletons do you have in your closet? It's still spring, after all—the perfect time for cleaning up and sweeping out old bones."

Carwyn thought about it for a moment and then asked, "Do you really want to hear about my skeletons, or are you just trying to be polite?"

"I want to hear about your skeletons."

"Okay."

So Carwyn told her about how he was the oldest of three and how, when he was twelve, his dad had been laid off from work, had started drinking, and then had been unable to stop drinking. Then his dad had moved on from hard liquor to hard drugs. He told her how his dad had burned through a lot of money his parents had in savings and then one day had just left. He was found dead of a drug overdose just a couple months later. Carwyn told Vivian that his mother was a smart and strong woman but hadn't been able to work much between his younger siblings' births.

Carwyn went on to tell Vivian that for a time after his father's passing, his mother and his two siblings had had to stay in shelters. He told her about how as soon as his mother was able, she had started working sixty-plus hours a week to put a roof over their heads and food on the table. He told Vivian about his dream to play professional soccer and how a lack of funds to play for select teams over the years and multiple injuries had kept him off the field. He finished by telling her, "So now my goal is to work for ESPN."

Perhaps it was because she felt more or less alone in the world. Perhaps it was because he was the first person who had really listened to her story. Whatever it was, Vivian felt an instant, natural connection to Carwyn, and she didn't want him to leave.

"I'm sorry to hear about what you went through, but I think it has made you a better, stronger person. I think we're both stronger people because of the unpleasant paths our lives have taken. And our paths have converged—another plus. But it's late, and I'm exhausted. That means it's time to turn this couch into a bed and for me to call it a night."

Carwyn stood up and helped Vivian fold out her futon. "Okay, so where should I meet you for lunch tomorrow?" he asked.

"We can figure that out tomorrow morning. I want you to stay tonight."

Carwyn was taken aback but managed to say, "Are you sure about that?"

"Absolutely."

Carwyn was pretty exhausted too, so he was grateful for the opportunity to avoid the long walk back to his hostel at almost five in the morning. Vivian went into the bathroom to brush her teeth. She came out in a longish T-shirt. It was loose and long enough to be a night shirt, but it was just short enough and just snug enough in certain strategic spots to be more than that to Carwyn's eyes.

Dear God, she's stunning, Carwyn thought.

"I have some mouthwash if you want to use it before bed."

"Thanks."

Carwyn gargled and made his way back out to the room. He stood there for a moment unsure of what to do or where to go.

"I'm not gonna bite, and the floor is certainly not very comfortable."

So Carwyn took off his jeans and shirt to sleep in his boxer briefs and undershirt. He climbed onto the futon, and Vivian inched right up beside him. Her hair smelled clean with a subtle but crisp, slightly fruity scent. Her legs against his were comfortably warm and smooth. Her feet were cold, but he didn't mind at all. In fact, in an odd way, he kind of liked her feet warming against his skin.

Almost instinctively, Vivian nuzzled her head into the natural resting place where Carwyn's chest, arm, and shoulder came together, and Carwyn slid his arm around her. His hand came to rest on her stomach just above her hip. His other hand came to rest on his own stomach. Vivian gently positioned one of her legs over Carwyn's, and she brought one of her arms up to Carwyn's stomach, where his hand was resting. She delicately, tentatively interlaced her fingers with his. It felt good and right to them both just to be there together, intertwined.

In a fatigue-softened voice, Vivian commented, "I'm very glad you're here, Carwyn."

"Me too."

Upon hearing Carwyn's response, Vivian snuggled even more firmly into his warm, strong, comforting body. The enervation of a long day caught up with them, and despite the magnetic force of their skin-to-skin contact, they both soon fell into a peaceful sleep.

— 24 —

ON A RAINY EVENING after business hours at a small, family-owned restaurant in New England, a decision was made. *The* decision was made. After extensive contemplation and surveillance, there was to be no more deliberating. A call was placed. *The* call was placed. The unfortunate bastard who had been in the wrong place at the wrong time was to be eliminated. It wasn't really his fault, of course, but he had to go nonetheless.

Even if all indications were that he hadn't yet said anything to anybody, that could all change when James Steele and Jack Freeman emerged into the political spotlight, and that would ruin everything. You could almost feel bad for the poor bastard. Almost.

— 25 —

WHEN CARWYN WOKE IN the afternoon he fleetingly experienced that where-am-I sensation that had recently become all too familiar. His tingling arm—it had gone to sleep thanks to Vivian's head—reminded him of where he was and of the night before. Vivian was not in the bed, but Carwyn assumed she was just in the bathroom. He lay there a moment, trying to immerse himself in her scent, which lingered in the sheets and on Vivian's pillow. He liked the way she smelled—not just her shampoo, not just her soap or her lotion, but *her*.

Carwyn didn't even wiggle or shake his arm out of some peculiar enjoyment he got from knowing that Vivian was the cause of his current case of pins and needles. *Wow, am I a goober or what?* he thought. When he had remained in the bed for so long that he could no longer discern Vivian's scent, he realized that she must be gone. He called out for her but got no reply.

He sat up, wondering where she had gone. Had she run off first thing, hoping that he would follow suit and leave, thus relieving her of any obligation of ever having to see him again? As he was thinking this, he became consciously aware that his arm was still asleep. He stood up and started to shake his arm ferociously, almost as if it were on fire. And it was at that precise moment that the door opened. Vivian, carrying a reusable shopping bag in one hand, just starred.

"Um."

"My arm went to sleep thanks to you," Carwyn explained.

A cute little giggle escaped her mouth, and Vivian replied, "Are you complaining?"

"No, not at all. What's in the bag?"

"Some goodies."

"What kind of goodies?"

"Just some stuff to eat."

"Does this mean no lunch date?"

"Well, it's almost one already, and I'm working tonight starting at seven, which means I have to be back here by five thirty at the latest to get ready.

And there are better things to do in Amsterdam on a nice day than eat lunch."

"Well, you'd know better than me, so let's eat your goodies."

With a coy smile, Vivian winked at Carwyn and said, "Then we'd never get out of here."

She removed a container of fresh berries, a small box that contained four small croissants, a jar of Nutella, two coffees, and two pear-shaped bottles of Orangina.

"I hope you don't mind a continental breakfast."

"Not at all, especially for lunch."

They ate and drank and chatted, and then Vivian shared her plans for the day. "Okay, so, I really want to take you to the Anne Frank House. You haven't already been, have you?" She didn't wait for an answer. "I've been there about a dozen times; it's where I go whenever my life seems to suck just a little bit too much. Going there really puts things in perspective for me, you know, and I leave with a renewed strength. Have you read the diary of Anne Frank?"

Carwyn actually thought for a very brief moment about saying he had, but he wasn't going to lie. "No."

"Isn't it like required reading in middle school?"

"Not for me, it wasn't."

"But you do know her story, right?"

"Yes, I do."

"Okay good, so we'll go, and then I want to take you to see the four narrowest houses in the world, a sort of Amsterdam canal front specialty. Oh, and I've got a large University of Amsterdam T-shirt you can wear if you don't want to wear the same thing you wore last night."

"Okay."

"You can leave your other shirt here."

Carwyn wondered why women were always scheming to acquire articles of men's clothing that they could later wear and claim as their own. When he put on the University of Amsterdam shirt, he couldn't help but think that it must have been another guy's shirt—a previous boyfriend's, maybe—and that thought struck him as oddly poignant.

Maybe life is just the pursuit of a girl that looks better in your clothes than you do. Sometimes you have to wear another man's clothes in the pursuit, and sometimes you lose the very shirt off your back in the pursuit. But with the right amount of luck and fashion sense, you'll find the right girl, the one who looks ready for the runway in a two-sizes-too-big royal cerulean button-up—and who won't run away.

"You ready?" Vivian asked after Carwyn had changed shirts.

"Yep."

They left, and Vivian led them to a bus stop. They got off the bus at the Westermarkt stop and walked the rest of the way to 263 Prinsengracht. From the outside, the historically significant house could have passed for any ordinary or insignificant canal house or office. The exterior walls appeared indistinctive. The windows were nondescript.

Inside, however, was much different, and looking out on the world from the nondescript windows, life seemed ever-so-subtly refracted. Even for Vivian, the view seemed different from ever before. *Sometimes it's not what you're looking at; it's who you're doing the looking with.* Vivian was happy, almost as if for the first time in her life.

About an hour later as they were leaving the ordinary-not-so-ordinary house, Carwyn noticed a thin trail of tears tracing their way down Vivian's cheek. He hesitated a moment but then gently wiped them away with his thumb.

"I'm sorry," Vivian said. "I always seem to end up crying when I come here—not from sadness but out of a sense of appreciation for what I have. This may sound strange, but I think sometimes beauty and tragedy are one and the same. Sometimes the more beautiful something is, the more tragic. Today this house seemed more tragic than ever, but that's because by seeing it with you it was more beautiful than ever. And I have more to appreciate than ever before. I guess my tears are a mixture of grief and joy. I guess it's all just a matter of perspective."

"You don't ever have to apologize for your emotions, at least not to me. Joy and sadness, beauty and pain aren't always opposites. I'm very glad you brought me here." Then to lighten the mood, Carwyn added, "Hell, I cried when the Jamaican bob sled team's sled broke in *Cool Runnings*. Of course, I was only about eight or nine at the time."

"That's cute."

"Oh good, I'm glad you think so. That's exactly what I was going for."

Picking up on his sarcasm, Vivian replied, "Cute is definitely not a bad thing, you know."

They decided to walk back from the Anne Frank house. As they made their way back toward the red light district, they stopped for Vivian to show Carwyn all the narrow houses she had mentioned. As they continued to walk and talk, Carwyn thought he saw a gleam in Vivian's eye. *Can you really see eye gleams?* he thought to himself.

In addition to Vivian's beautiful brown eyes, Carwyn took pleasurable notice of her soft, full lips and the adorable smile they formed as she spoke. He wanted to stop the world and kiss her right then and there. He was aware that he was staring at her lips, and he even felt as if his body was being pulled in that direction—as if Vivian's lips had their own gravitational pull. Unsure of himself, Carwyn defied the gravitational laws of Vivian's lips and did not follow through with a kiss.

Vivian must have perceived (and shared) Carwyn's yearning, for she stopped walking, met his lips with hers, and kissed him fully but fleetingly. The kiss, which seemed to singe their very breaths with a most deliciously welcome and fervent heat, was but a brief meeting of eager lips. "Well," Vivian interposed, "I have to head home to get ready, but maybe you'd be interested in meeting me after work again tonight. I still have your shirt."

"I'd like that. What time?"

"Just come right at two."

"Okay. I'll see you then."

"I'll be looking forward to it."

I'll be looking forward to it. As Carwyn reflected on Vivian's parting comment and on their afternoon together, a smile took full control of his lips. The feeling he had now was nothing like the tingly feeling Karolina had given him in Sweden. That had been a purely physical reaction. This was much more encompassing. It was mental, emotional, physical, even spiritual. It was like the smile that had taken control of his lips had taken over his entire being. It was as if he was high, and Vivian was the perfect drug.

— 26 —

IN THE PARISIAN TWILIGHT, Bret and Rebecca sat on a quaint terrace. They had a postcard-worthy view of the city, the Seine, and the Eiffel Tower all lit up in the distance. It was their last night in Paris. They enjoyed an exquisite meal and drank even better wine. The price of their meal was a result not only of its quality but also the celebrity of the chef preparing it and the location of the restaurant. The cost of the wine was a product of the vineyard that had produced it.

The vineyard was small, but had a reputation *sans égal*. Its wine was served in only the finest restaurants in France. The expensive bottle from which Bret and Rebecca were drawing their warm wine buzz was from a special lot, not so much made or produced as crafted by the vineyard. It was the result of a divine union between art and science.

The vineyard used three varietals of choice grapes, received the input of the most renowned sommeliers of France and Italy, and spent three times as long throughout the entire winemaking process in order to imbue it with, as the vineyard expressed it, *"La coeur et la nature mêmes du raisin; l'amour, la passion, et le charme romantique de toute la France; l'esprit des rois; et le souffle de Dieu."* ("The very heart and nature of the grape; the love, the passion, and the romance of all France; the spirit of kings; and the breath of God.")

There was more than one trade secret at the heart of the wine's production to which no more than three or four living people were privy. It was as perfect a wine as could be conjured or crafted, almost as if one of the unknown ingredients was some subtly powerful drug. Its scarcity and label, as much as its flawless aroma, sweetness, acidity, tannin quality, balance, and body, gave rise to its high price tag.

The wine that Bret and Rebecca were drinking, referred to simply as *trois*, was a masterpiece of consumable art perfected by nature, intuition, and science. Bret felt as if he could taste history, divinity, royalty, sexuality in every drop, almost as if he were some *haute monde* vampire drinking the blood of kings or a distinguished guest at the last supper sipping on the blood of Christ.

And for Rebecca, one of the unknown ingredients really was a subtly powerful drug.

*   *   *   *

She looked as if should would have the power to get away with anything—with murder even. She had such a raw beauty and sexual energy about her that it was quite inconceivable that any man, regardless of his sexuality, could resist her advances. She looked as if she would never have to pay for anything in her life. She looked as if every government on the planet would want her working for them, because she would have the ability to seduce and elicit information from anybody in the world, male or female. And she looked like she would enjoy it.

Bret had met Alexis somewhat recently in Atlantic City, and he was most certainly unable to resist her advances. They had crazy, dirty, nasty sex, and there was nothing that Alexis would not do. The rougher, nastier, or more taboo it was, the more she seemed to like it. Because their perversions had been so in sync, Bret and Alexis had exchanged cell numbers. They texted lewd and extreme ideas to each other somewhat regularly. Since Alexis lived only a couple of hours away in Providence, Rhode Island, they had gotten together for nasty sexual sessions twice since their first encounter.

When Alexis texted Bret, "I wish I could deepthroat you atop the Eiffel Tower," he responded, "I have a spectacular view of the Eiffel Tower from my hotel suite." Upon the discovery that they were both in Paris, they made plans to go—that very night—to an underground sex club Alexis had recently discovered.

Throughout the day, Bret and Alexis had planned their depraved tryst, and Alexis even told Bret what he could slip into Rebecca's drink to knock her out for about five hours.

*   *   *   *

Bret barely got Rebecca back to the hotel room before she passed out. Once back in the overpriced room, Bret got Rebecca out of her clothes and hoisted her into the bed. Bret watched Rebecca for just a few seconds to make sure she was really out of it. She was. Completely. A

103

train could have crashed right into the room, and Rebecca would not have woken up. Satisfied that he would have more than enough time for his raunchy rendezvous, Bret quickly exited the room with a smirk on his face.

27

CARWYN WOKE UP IN his bunk and almost rolled right off—again. He had taken the top bunk because he preferred to be the late-to-bed asshole that woke up his bunk mate rather than the other way around. Not that he actually wanted to be an asshole; he just really didn't want to be the asshol*ee*. Carwyn got out of bed and freshened up. He felt surprisingly alert given how little sleep he'd had recently. Maybe it had something to do with getting to see Vivian again.

Vivian was smart, funny, sincere, and had the perfect proportions of moxy and vulnerability. Carwyn was beyond excited; he was damn near giddy. He felt like a school kid. He was half skipping as he made his way toward Vivian's window. He seriously wondered if it was possible to have gotten a secondhand high from his hostel, because he was genuinely contemplating the symbolism of having first made Vivian's acquaintance through a window.

This Canadian expatriate prostitute had seemingly beguiled him, but in such a way that he was not one bit wary or cynical about the circumstances or about his beguilement at her hands (and eyes, and hair, and nose, and arms, and legs, and breasts, and butt, and feet, and lips, and hell, even her teeth). Carwyn was simply appreciative of the weightlessness he felt. It was as if he was gliding, not just skipping, across the street to the window where he would meet Vivian, being gently wafted there by a cool, crisp, delicate Dutch breeze.

Carwyn felt as if he got to the window almost without expending any effort whatsoever. He felt a little silly and even somewhat crazy about how excited he was to see Vivian. He found himself contemplating Friedrich Nietzsche: "There is always some madness in love. But there is also always some reason in madness." But surely he didn't love Vivian? He'd only just met her.

At that very moment, they didn't matter: love, like, lust, loneliness, left out, liberated, or any other *L* word, *didn't* matter. There was no need for labels, especially premature labels, for Carwyn to simply live and enjoy his life in this moment. He felt like some cheesy motivational poster beseeching the masses to live out loud or laugh or some other such superfluous shibboleth. But he didn't care.

Vivian was standing just across the street, waiting for him. She looked beautiful in the moonlight, just as she had in the sunlight, just as she had in red light, and inevitably, just as she would look in neon light, or firelight, or even by flashlight.

Carwyn had always found the notion of someone glowing to be rather odd. He figured that a human being figuratively glowing couldn't be very flattering based on the reality that any human being who was literally glowing would be positively scary or quite creepy. Carwyn had no delusions or misconceptions that Vivian was either figuratively or literally glowing. Perhaps she was beaming. Perhaps she even looked perfectly angelic (because, although it was somewhat contradictory to the reality of how they had met, *angelic* had no creepy parallel literalisms). But she was not glowing. That would just be silly. Carwyn quickened his pace.

"Hi," he said as he approached.

"Hey you. How are ya?"

"I'm excellent; how are you?"

"Well, today was a long day. I couldn't wait to see you!"

"Seriously?"

"Seriously."

"Well, I'm flattered. So is it off to McDonald's for some vegetarian croquets?"

"Funny, but I already ate. I thought we could just chat, maybe play some go fish."

"Go fish? As in the card game?"

"Yep."

"Seriously?"

"Seriously. Why, too juvenile for you?"

"No, not at all. I love playing cards. I just haven't played go fish in forever."

"Perfect."

They walked to Vivian's apartment hand in hand, at one point even skipping for about half a block.

Vivian took a quick shower and emerged in sweatpants and a

T-shirt, still incomparably (bordering on incomprehensibly) beautiful. She made some hot chocolate and brought a mug to Carwyn. When she got out the playing cards, she playfully commented, "I hope you're not a poor loser."

Vivian dealt the cards, and she and Carwyn drank their hot chocolate and played go fish. Carwyn found it hard to concentrate on the game. The Dutch hot chocolate was probably the best he had ever had (not that he was a big hot chocolate drinker). More distractingly, Vivian was adorably gorgeous, and she just smelled so damn good. *That shampoo should seriously be illegal.* He wanted to kiss her again, this time for much longer than before.

"Do you have any tens?" he asked.

"Go fish."

"Do you have any threes?"

"Damn," he said.

Vivian laughed as he handed over his threes. She quickly won the game.

"I think you were cheating," Carwyn declared, feigning righteous indignation.

"Oh? And how did I manage to accomplish cheating at go fish?"

"You distracted me."

"How did I distract you?"

"By sitting there."

"Sitting wh—"

But Vivian's question was cut off by Carwyn's lips. He couldn't hold back any longer, and he pressed his lips to hers in a deep, passionate, kiss. The brief warmth from earlier in the day was boiling over now. An electric heat rippled from their lips through their bodies and coursed through their veins. It was an unexpected, uninhibited connection. They allowed their mouths to open ever so slightly and their tongues to taste one another's lips and the hint of chocolate on each other's tongues.

Carwyn thought Vivian's lips seemed to taste not just of chocolate but also of cinnamon and cotton candy. Vivian could taste sweet and salty honey and cherry in Carwyn's kiss. Of course, other than chocolate and a dash of cinnamon, these flavors weren't actually present on either Vivian's or Carwyn's lips or tongue or breath. Still, it was as if they were two rare and transcendent sommeliers discerning, differentiating, appraising, and savoring all the subtle intricacies of a spirit more divine than anything derived from any fermented fruit.

Carwyn stood, and Vivian stood with him, their lips never parting. As they stood, still kissing, teasing, tasting, engaging, Carwyn managed to unfold the futon. Then he guided Vivian back down. Carwyn finally broke the connection between their lips. As their lips continued to simmer with longing, Carwyn removed his shirt and then pulled Vivian's shirt off over her head. As she had dressed for bed after her shower, Vivian was not wearing a bra. Her nipples were pert with excitement. Carwyn removed his jeans and Vivian's sweatpants. Once he removed her underwear, Vivian was completely naked.

As Carwyn removed his boxer briefs, revealing to Vivian his complete state of arousal, she seemed to tense up ever so slightly. Now that they were both naked and the reality of the situation was apparent, she seemed nervous. This at first made no sense to Carwyn, but then he realized why her nervousness made complete and perfect sense.

When Vivian was working, she was not only playing a part but was ultimately in charge. Here, now, with Carwyn in her apartment, her home, she was no longer fully in charge. She was vulnerable. Carwyn respected her timidity. He took Vivian's right hand in his and kissed it, and then he moved toward Vivian so that his lips could once again meet hers. As they continued to kiss, their heart rates elevated, pounding out an ancient rhythm. Their breathing became more rapid and deep. When their skin touched, a current seemed to dance in, among, between, and all around them.

Then Vivian half-whispered, "Thank you."

Carwyn didn't know exactly what she was thanking him for or how he might possibly respond to such a statement, so he remained silent. A moment passed. In between kisses, Carwyn commented, "I've never felt such intensity in a kiss. I want to touch you, taste you, feel you … all over."

Vivian looked into Carwyn's eyes, and when he met her passionate gaze, she said, "Will you make love to me slowly?"

"That is exactly what I want to do."

"And I know this is so, so stupid, but no condom. I want to feel you, skin to skin."

Carwyn knew it was stupid too, having unprotected sex with a prostitute, but he gently positioned Vivian on her back before positioning himself over her. He adjusted his body so that they were lined up just so. He could feel how excessively wet she was, and with his right hand he guided himself to the opening between her legs. He let his body inch closer to hers, and his own weight provided the perfect amount of force with which to enter her fully. As his body came all the way down to touch hers, he moved deep into her, and they both let out gasps of pleasure, affection, and desire. In the moment after Carwyn first entered Vivian, it felt as if, not only had he never had sex with *her* before, but as if it was his first time being intimate with *anyone*. He had previously thought that such a sensation was only a myth.

It was a beautiful paradox, to be sure, or maybe just a contradiction in action—a prostitute and a previous customer gently fumbling over each other like nervous first-time lovers as they brought their bodies into a slow, deep, intimate rhythm.

After some immeasurable amount of time, Carwyn sat up, bringing Vivian up onto his lap with her legs wrapped around his lower back. They moved and rocked back and forth slowly, at times so slowly that one might not have been able to discern any motion at all with the naked eye. As they moved, flexing and contracting muscles, they looked each other in the eyes, kissing gently and caressing each other.

Time seemed to lose all meaning. Vivian and Carwyn had been making love for who knows how long, quietly enjoying each other, when Vivian let out a distinctive soft moan.

"You okay?" asked Carwyn.

"I don't think I've ever been better. I'm close."

"To coming?"

"Yes, but I don't want you to move any harder or faster. I want to come just like this, moving slowly, holding on to you."

"Okay. Do you think you can control it? Because I want to come with you."

"At the same time?"

"Yes. Think we can do it?"

"We can try."

And so, because they were now exerting effort to reach climax in sublime orgasmic unison yet were moving with the same pace and force and rhythm, the sensations flowing through their bodies as they moved in synergistic harmony together grew exponentially more intense. Vivian concentrated on her body and on bringing the intimate sexual climb to the precipice. She focused and flexed and adjusted their rhythm ever so slightly.

"Carwyn, I'm right there. Are you?"

"Yes, I'm close; don't hold back."

As they rocked, wrapped up tight in each other, they looked intently into each other's eyes and, without any more words, announced to each other that their bodies were at the point of no return. They reached climax simultaneously.

The flood gates of euphoria opened, and waves of high-voltage sensation surged through them both. They were still holding each other, and they both experienced the power of a joint sensation. With every heartbeat, waves of pleasure pulsed through them both, from one to the other and back again. As they continued to hold on to each other, the echoes of sensations continued to ripple through their bodies until finally they lay back to together, still embracing, still searching one another's faces and eyes, discerning specks of color—a tiny fleck of gold weaved with an even smaller speck of green on a blue iris here, a perfectly placed brown freckle there—likely never before noticed by any other person.

Vivian broke their blissful silence by breathily whispering, "That is without a doubt the single most amazing, pleasure-filled, intimate, truly wonderful sensation I have ever had in my entire life by far."

"I think, if possible, that may be an understatement."

Tired, and never having felt more comforted, secure, and relaxed, Carwyn and Vivian fell asleep wrapped up in each other's arms just as the sun was starting to rise and paint a brand new day.

— 28 —

THE NEXT MORNING, CARWYN woke first. He watched Vivian sleep for several minutes. He felt a little creepy, but it was hard not to look at her. Did her face look like some airbrushed picture out of a magazine? No, of course not. There were the minor flaws that any real human being has. Carwyn didn't want to disturb Vivian, so he tried to go back to sleep. After about five minutes of lying there with his eyes closed, he could feel Vivian nuzzle into him, evidence that she too was at least partially awake.

"Good morning," he said.

"Oh, you're up. I hope I didn't wake you with my, um, burrowing. Good morning."

"Nope, you didn't wake me. Are you working today?"

"Only if you don't want to spend the day with me."

"So it's completely up to me, huh? Well, I'd like to spend the day with you."

"Well then, it's settled. That was easy." She rolled over on top of him and kissed him.

"I want to feel you inside me again," she said, "but we should get going."

"Get going?"

"Yeah, we have a full day ahead of us."

"We do, do we? So that whole bit about spending the day with you was all for show, huh??"

"Yeah, sorry. But hey, I think you should go check out of your hostel and bring all your stuff back here to stay for the rest of your trip—if you want to, of course. I'll shower and get ready while you're gone. Then you can shower here when you get back."

"Well, yes ma'am." Carwyn left Vivian's apartment and walked as quickly as he could back to his hostel, thinking about the night before and Vivian's invitation. *Maybe Nietzsche was right*, he thought. *Could this serendipitous encounter with a Canadian prostitute in Amsterdam be the beginning of my last relationship? Is all this just mad enough to be the beginning of something lasting?*

As he made his way up to his shared room and got his things together, his mind raced. The only thing he knew for certain was that he sure didn't mind so much that Bret wasn't around getting him drunk anymore. As he shoved all his belongings into his bag, he noticed that it looked like his stuff had been rifled through. He ignored it and ran down the stairs to check out. *So what if somebody stole a pair of my jeans or even my favorite shirt?*

After checking out of the hostel, Carwyn decided to take a cab back to Vivian's place. When he got there he pushed the button for Vivian's apartment, and she buzzed him in. He ran up the stairs and knocked. She met him at the door with a kiss. Once he was inside the apartment and had put his stuff down, Carwyn asked, "So where are we headed today?"

"I'll tell you after you're showered and ready to go."

"Okay," he said and headed into the bathroom to shower. About ten minutes later, Carwyn emerged from the bathroom wearing only a towel.

"If you want to go anywhere today, you better hurry up and get dressed before I decide to forgo my plans and stay in bed with you all day."

"Well, would that be such a bad thing?"

"No, it wouldn't, but it's such a beautiful day, and there will be time for laying in bed tonight."

"Okay, so where are we going?"

"The Hague. Despite everything, it's one of my favorite cities. I'd like to take you there to create some pleasant new memories. It's only about forty-five minutes, and we can cuddle on the train."

Vivian was grinning from ear to ear, and Carwyn couldn't help but think about what it might be like seeing that smile for the rest of his life. Just seeing her smiling and happy made him feel bulletproof—or something equally as cheesy. "Sounds perfect to me," he said.

Carwyn picked out some clothes from his bag and quickly got dressed. They left Vivian's apartment and walked hand in hand to Amsterdam Centraal. Vivian purchased her ticket, and they boarded the next train to The Hague. They only had to wait about five minutes.

Vivian proclaimed that she enjoyed The Hague so much because it was the international city of peace and justice. She had quite a lot of information to share. Beyond sharing her tour-guide level of knowledge, Vivian took Carwyn on a tour of a number of the important international legal organizations in the city.

Carwyn's feet were definitely starting to hurt, although he didn't really mind. He was perfectly happy to traipse all over The Hague, stopping by all the places Vivian wanted to show him. Carwyn found himself wondering if he was enjoying his sightseeing tour for its own sake or if his enjoyment was derived vicariously from Vivian's visible happiness at showing off some of her favorite places. He knew one thing: if it was important to her, it was important to him.

One place that Carwyn felt pretty sure he would have enjoyed even in the absence of his vicarious happiness was the Madurodam. The Madurodam had absolutely nothing to do with international law. The Madurodam was a miniature city that contained hundreds of scale models of Dutch landmarks in a miniature Dutch landscape. As they were walking through the miniature city, Carwyn decided to make himself an impromptu giant, clomping through the miniature streets. Vivian could not readily decide whether she should or shouldn't feel embarrassed, but the lighthearted cuteness of Carwyn's antics won her over. She even played along for a brief moment. The funny looks they got from men, women, and children didn't faze them at all. They both felt ten feet tall.

As they were leaving the Madurodam, Vivian said, "I hope I haven't bored you today, taking you to so many unexciting places."

"You know," Carwyn replied, "I don't know if I would ever have come here on my own or gone to all the places we went to today, but everything you've shown me and told me about has been extremely fascinating, and seeing it all with you, just being with you, has been anything but boring. I'm very glad you brought me here; today has been a great day. I just wish there were more hours in the day to spend with you."

But the day was indeed coming to an end. Twilight appeared eager to overtake the dimming Dutch daylight. Wisps of orange and rose were starting to flirt with the scattered clouds in the sky.

"I know a great little place for dinner. They've got great desserts, and we'll be pretty close to the train station when we're done."

"Lead the way, my beautiful tour guide."

Vivian grabbed Carwyn's hand, and, quite contentedly, they walked in silence for several blocks. Carwyn wondered what Vivian was thinking about as they ambled hand in hand. He was contemplating the randomness and the mystery of human connections and interaction. Vivian, who was also wondering what Carwyn was thinking, was silently reveling in how wondrous it was to feel content and at peace for the first time in a very long time.

The silence as the pair reflected on their happiness was not awkward. It was not boring. It was not unpleasant in any way. It was as if for just a short while Vivian and Carwyn were one, floating to their next destination, unaware and unfazed by the goings-on around them.

29

FOR BRET, MONTE CARLO was almost a complete bust. The flight from Orly in Paris to Côte-d'Azur International in Nice and then the helicopter flight to Monte Carlo were both miserable because of Rebecca's sedative hangover. It was Grand Prix weekend, so the approximately three-thousand-inhabitant administrative area of the Principality of Monaco was teeming (overrun, really) with spectators and tourists. Bret had no idea how Rebecca got a room at the world-famous Hôtel de Paris.

On top of the crowds, the games at Le Grand Casino de Monte-Carlo (European roulette, chemin de fer, blackjack, and punto banco) were not really Bret's cup of tea. The only tables where he didn't lose were the blackjack tables. Even counting his meager winnings at those tables, Bret definitely ended up in the hole.

The saving grace for Bret was the dinning experience at Louis XV. The Mediterranean sea bass was to die for, and being able to select a wine from the world's largest wine cellar was a definite plus. Getting to nail Rebecca in one of *Les Supers Privés* gaming rooms was also nice—as, of course, was taking the twenty-minute train ride to Nice in order to have every inch of Alexis for seconds.

—— 30 ——

CARWYN DIDN'T WANT TO leave Vivian's little shoebox in Amsterdam, but he had resigned himself to the fact that as much as he wanted his time with Vivian to go on indefinitely, it was inevitably going to come to an end. Since it was going to come to an end, Carwyn figured that he should at least give himself one day in Moscow to enjoy the city before his flight home. If he didn't, he'd surely regret it later. Carwyn intended to invite Vivian to come along, but he assumed she would decline.

He would have to book a flight, since a train ride would have been about a thirty-hour venture. It was on the train ride back from The Hague to Amsterdam that Carwyn mentioned his impending departure.

"But it seems like you just got here, and I just began spending time with you."

"I know, but my flight home is from Moscow, and I do want to see the city for one day before I head home. I would love to see it with you, if you're able to come with me."

"I would love to go, but I guess my going with you is just as impractical as you staying with me."

"Yeah, I guess it is pretty impractical," Carwyn replied, "but I don't want to lose touch with you. I—"

"Well, I'm not just gonna forget that you exist. I don't think I could, even if I tried. We're obviously going to exchange numbers and e-mail addresses. And there's always Facebook."

Carwyn took a brief moment to calculate what to say next and to calculate if he really wanted to say it. "Viv …" It was the first time he had shortened her name (the first step to a pet name) and as simple and insignificant as it might have been, Carwyn was still surprised to hear himself utter the pre-pet name. "I, uh, well … I'm just gonna say it. I want you to come visit me in Boston. I'd even pick you up at the airport."

"Well, I can promise I'll call and e-mail you, but I can't promise a trip anytime soon. There would just be so much emotional baggage associated with being so close to home."

Carwyn felt defeated, dejected—rejected. He felt empty inside. He was sure that in spite of his best efforts to remain neutral on the outside, his dejection was readily apparent on his face. If Vivian had picked up on the confession in Carwyn's expression, she did not let on.

"Okay," Carwyn said after what seemed to him to be too long of a pause, "I guess I have to take what I can get. You think you can help me get a cheap plane ticket?"

"Sure. We can do an internet search tonight. I'll use a Dutch site that might find cheaper prices than an American site."

"Great, thanks."

"You're welcome. And just so you know, my hesitancy to travel to America has nothing to do with you."

After the digression into Carwyn's travel plans, the pair fell back into more pleasant conversation for the rest of the train ride, but Carwyn just couldn't shake off his empty feeling.

Night had fully descended by the time they arrived at Amsterdam Centraal. Vivian new a place to rent English-language movies. They rented a recently released comedy and headed back to Vivian's place. They watched the movie on Vivian's laptop and laughed in unison, but their laughter was ever so subtly stunted by the weight of impending separation that hung in the air.

Neither one mentioned Carwyn's departure again. They were both tired after their long day, so after the movie they folded out Vivian's futon and hopped into bed. They made love with desperate intensity, as if it would allow them to hold on to one another longer and beat back time. As dynamic and pure and almost transcendent as they were together, they were not omnipotent.

The effortlessly harmonic pair was happy in the moment, and disregarding the diamondlike beads of sweat they had mined from each other during their passionate lovemaking, they folded into each other. Sleep came quickly. Still, Carwyn couldn't help but think as he fell into an imperfect slumber that he was not altogether unlike a prisoner on death row.

— 31 —

AENEID HAD BEEN DISPATCHED to deal with Bret Hightower. The *gentiluomini privati* had, through their network of connections, developed and put in motion a grand plan that they would simply not allow to be jeopardized in any way.

The *gentiluomini privati* were grooming two candidates, one Republican and one Democrat, for either the 2020 or the 2024 presidential election. It was a project that had originated as a drunken conversation between Jonny and a New Hampshire state representative after a long night of cards. The project had actually begun in 2009 after President Obama took office. The *gentiluomini* wanted to ensure that for at least four years, regardless of which party won the election, they would have some measure of influence over the recognized leader of the free world.

One of the hand-picked candidates-to-be was James Reagan Steele (named, in part, after the fortieth president of the United States, Ronald Reagan). Steele was a forty-two-year-old white Democrat from South Carolina. He was married to a woman with a Mexican mother and a white father.

The other candidate-to-be was Jack Robinson Freeman (named after baseball legend Jackie Robinson). Freeman, forty-six, was a black Republican from New York. Freeman was married to a woman who could at least allegedly trace her roots back to Isabella Baumfree (better known as Sojourner Truth).

The two were perfect in almost every way. They had presidential looks. They had presidential names. They had picture-perfect families. They had impeccable voting records. But if either one had been completely perfect, then the *gentiluomini's* plan would have been flawed from the outset. They each needed a major skeleton in the closet for the *gentiluomini's* plan to work, and they each had one.

The only real political liability for Jack was that, despite having been married to a wonderful woman for twelve years and having three great children, he was gay. He was gay, and he didn't want anyone to know it.

The only political liability for James was that he cheated on his wife, often with girls ranging in age from fifteen to seventeen. He wasn't exactly a pedophile, but he did have a compulsion, and he was certainly cutting it damn close.

Now these political liabilities were exactly what the *gentiluomini* wanted. The fact that James and Jack were (almost) perfect president material, each with but one major skeleton in his closet, was exactly how the *gentiluomini* intended to make their plan work—as long as they controlled the information.

It was control over each candidate's private information that gave the *gentiluomini* their power. Essentially, the plan was to get both James and Jack nominated and then exert their influence from that point on to get what they wanted. The *gentiluomini* had pulled the puppet strings and controlled and contained the information about both candidates for a couple of years. Everything was progressing in just the way they had hoped.

But then information about Jack's proclivities became decontained. Two unfortunate individuals had seen something they should not have seen. One, a vagrant that nobody would miss, had been disposed of immediately. The other happened to be Bret Hightower. It was doubtful that either even knew the significance of what he had seen, but that was a risk the *gentiluomini private* were simply not going to take.

If the information was disseminated, the *gentiluomini's* plan would fail. They could not allow that. After investigating whether and to what extent Bret had in any way recorded or passed on the information, he too was to be disposed of. And that was precisely where Aeneid came in. She knew her assignment, and she knew how to carry it out. The only questions that remained now were precisely when and where she would complete the task.

— 32 —

Vivian politely declined the invitation to accompany Carwyn to the airport. She had helped him book a cheap ticket the night before, and she preferred to say her good-byes on her terms, not as dictated by flight schedules and security protocols.

They had gotten up early. They did not make love, which Carwyn and Vivian both regretted and cherished at the same time. Instead of making love, they sat tangled up in each other until it was time for Carwyn to leave. Although Vivian was the one, despite her best efforts, to shed a few tears, it would have been a hard sell to convince Carwyn that he was any less miserable. He felt as if he had an almost symbiotic connection with Vivian, and now, by his very own actions, he was quite possibly severing that connection.

Although it probably was not yet a completely accurate statement, both Carwyn and Vivian wanted to say, "I love you." They both fought off the urge but certainly not because they didn't feel it in those last moments together. Their final hug and kiss were at once uplifting, fulfilling, and down right depressing.

From the moment Carwyn could no longer view Vivian's building from his cab, he felt strikingly, desperately hollow. It was nothing like the view from the cab window in Stockholm as he had sped away from Karolina's house. From somewhere in his consciousness, he could practically hear himself screaming out to the cab driver to turn around, but Carwyn's adamant thoughts never translated into any audible articulation. Before he even had a chance to think fully about what he was doing, Carwyn was at the airport, and then he was on a plane to Moscow.

From the time Carwyn got off the plane at Domodedovo International Airport, he only had about twenty-nine hours in Moscow before his flight home. After he checked into his hostel, Carwyn immediately hit the streets to take in as much of the city as he could.

His first destination was the first destination of many a tourist: Red Square in the heart of Moscow.

After some whirlwind sightseeing, Carwyn made his way down Old Arbat Street. Other than *"Da,"* he didn't know a single word of Russian, and his inability to decipher any helpful amount of the language both unsettled and excited him. After enjoying an overpriced meal, he almost purchased a vastly overpriced souvenir for Vivian. Carwyn missed Vivian, hauntingly so, more than he had ever missed another human being. *Madness*, he thought.

On his walk back to his hostel, he was overcome by an odd lonely feeling. He wanted to share his experience with Vivian. With mixed emotions, he thought, *There is nothing so beautiful in this world that it would not be rendered all the more beautiful by seeing it through four eyes instead of just two*, and he felt very poetic. *I guess we all just need the right muse.*

When he got back to his hostel, he noticed a flyer for a bar crawl that he had not noticed when he checked in. It was specifically geared for English speakers and promised to highlight some of Moscow's best drinking establishments. There were six planned stops on the crawl. The flyer even had the price listed in U.S. dollars. Carwyn asked the girl at the desk about it and decided it would be the best way to experience the city at night. The bar crawl left from his hostel at nine o'clock.

Carwyn hoped it would be worth the forty bucks he had shelled out, but he didn't quite know what might make it worth it. He had no interest in picking someone up.

Carwyn got to the meeting spot several minutes before nine. A small crowd was gathered. The crowd was made up of an almost equal number of men and women, and there were four guides there to lead the bar crawl. The first bar was only about two blocks away, the second was pretty close to the first, the third was about a half-mile walk from the second, the fourth was right next door to the third, and the fifth was several blocks from the fourth. The sixth and final stop was at a two-story club.

*   *   *   *

Carwyn walked down a completely unfamiliar street. It was light outside. He had a more apprehensive, almost foreboding, feeling than what often accompanied the memory gaps resulting from blacking out.

Where the hell am I? Where the hell have I been? Almost reflexively, he reached for his wallet. It was still there. With an anxious, uneasy feeling, he opened it. His driver's license and credit card were there. However, all Bret's business cards were gone, and so was all Carwyn's cash. *Shit.* He didn't know exactly how much total cash he had lost, but he did remember that there had been sixty dollars he had never exchanged. A nervous panic started to set in. The last thing he could remember was getting onto the subway to go to the last bar. *Why would we take the subway to the last bar? How dumb is that?* He had no recollection of the last bar at all. And what on earth would he have spent his unexchanged cash on? *That can't be good.*

Next Carwyn checked his cell phone to see what time it was. It was seven in the morning. He checked his call history and text log. He had made no outgoing calls. He had, however, sent four texts to Vivian: "Hi!" at 11:03 p.m.; "I wish uwere here" at 11:57 p.m.; "I missd yoi" at 1:18 a.m.; and "I tjink i am lost i wis i was lost withu" at 2:09 a.m.

After reading his drunk texts, he felt the sting of embarrassment. He had received seven texts from Vivian: "Hi back, babe :)" at 11:11 p.m.; "I wish I was there with you too!" at 11:58 p.m.; "Carwyn, are you drunk or something?" at 1:27 a.m.; "Want me to call and help you navigate?" at 2:11 a.m.; "Carwyn, answer your phone!" at 2:36 a.m.; "Carwyn, call or text me back. I am worried!" at 3:02 a.m.; and "Carwyn, this is not funny call me as soon as you get my messages i am seriously freaking out now!!" at 3:44 a.m.

There were also three missed calls from Vivian. She had left two messages. The first message was from around 2:25 a.m.: "Carwyn, hey babe, just calling to help you find your way home. If you are drunk and lost in Moscow, you might never find your way. Call me when you get this, babe." The second message had been left at 3:53 a.m.: "Carwyn, if you aren't already dead, I am personally going to fly to Russia and kill you. I am worried sick over here. I can't sleep. My stomach hurts. Please, please call me as soon as you can. I miss you so much."

Carwyn's embarrassment was now accompanied by guilt. He felt awful. He loved hearing the sound of Vivian's voice and that she had called him babe (she hadn't called him that while he was in Amsterdam), but he felt like a gigantic asshole for worrying her. He dialed her number right away.

"Hello," answered a very sleepy sounding Vivian.

"Vivian, it's Carwyn. I am so sorry about last night. I don't know what happened."

"Carwyn," she said, sounding more relieved than angry or annoyed, "are you okay? I was up all night worrying about you. Finally I just had to drink an entire bottle of wine to help me sleep."

"Yes, I'm okay. My wallet's empty, but I'm alive, and I still have all my organs."

"Well, that's good to hear … but babe, now that I know you're alive, I have really got to try and get some more sleep. Will you call me later?"

"Yes, I will."

"Okay, good. I miss you. I'm glad you're okay."

"I miss you too. Is that crazy?"

"I don't think so. Do you think it's crazy?"

"No, I guess not. But even if it is crazy, I don't care."

Vivian laughed a cute, tired laugh. "I like the sound of that," she said, "but don't scare me like that again, okay, ya big jerk?"

"Okay. Hey, by the way, your tired voice sounds absolutely adorable, but I'll let you get back to sleep now. And I'll talk to you later, Viv."

"Talk to you later, babe."

When Carwyn hung up, he had a smile on his face. He really liked being Vivian's babe.

Carwyn momentarily forgot about the mysteries of the night before as he refocused his concentration on getting back to his hostel. Although he didn't feel hungover in the traditional sense—maybe because he had never been to sleep—his entire body felt drained and weak. He was in dire need of sleep. He picked a direction and started walking. He had no idea whether he was walking toward or away from his hostel.

He walked and walked. He had no money for a taxi. To make matters worse, he didn't remember the name of his hostel, so he couldn't even attempt to ask for directions. *Shit, why didn't I get Vivian to help me?* But he wasn't about to call her back now and disturb her again.

Finally Carwyn saw something he thought he recognized. He went with his gut, but still his hostel and the welcome haven of his crappy little cot were nowhere to be seen. Just before nine o'clock in the morning, Carwyn finally spotted his hostel, basically by complete accident. He was beyond relieved to find that he still had his key card to his mixed-gender dormitory-style room, but he was absolutely pissed at himself for not thinking to look on the key card for the address or at least the name of the hostel—because it had the name.

He went directly to his room and directly to his cot. When Carwyn hit the flat, moderately soft surface, physiology took over, and he passed out in about ten seconds.

Upon waking, Carwyn felt okay at first. Since his nightmarishly long flight home departed in just under three hours, he immediately took a quick shower and packed up all his stuff. When he went to check out, the same Russian girl who had sold him on the bar crawl was there.

"Check out is at one," she said, "but no worry. I will not charge you late check-out fee."

"Thank you," Carwyn managed to say.

"Welcome," said the nameless girl in her sexy Russian accent. "You hav'd fun last night?"

Being completely honest, Carwyn replied, "I think so."

"Maybe too much vodka?"

"Maybe. Do you know where I can get a taxi to the airport?"

"Domodedovo?"

"Yes."

"I will call."

"Thank you."

"*Pa-zhal-sta*," she said. Carwyn could only assume it meant "you're welcome".

The friendly Russian girl was obnoxiously sexy, but Carwyn's recognition of the fact was objective. He felt no subjective attraction to her. He decided to wait outside for the taxi. Outside, Carwyn suddenly felt shame for getting blackout drunk the night before. His shame, however, was mixed with a sinking, almost sickening feeling of dread. He somehow knew something bad had happened, but he had no idea what.

On top of his emotional state, Carwyn felt like a giant pile of shit physically. He did not have a headache. He was not nauseous. However, his whole body felt like it was literally shutting down. He felt so weak that he simply could no longer stand. He collapsed to the ground flat on his back. He wondered if this was what it felt like when someone was dying. He thought momentarily that he actually *was* dying.

Lying helpless on the ground helped some. Lying there feeling both physically and psychologically unwell, he missed Vivian. Again. A lot. He wished he was flying back to her instead of back home. He briefly wondered what Bret had been up to the past few days, but his mind went right back to Vivian. He almost fell asleep right there on the ground, but luckily the taxi pulled up and honked just before he lapsed back into a coma.

The taxi driver got out and asked simply, "Domodedovo?" When Carwyn said yes, the driver grabbed Carwyn's luggage and put it in the trunk. Carwyn sprawled out in the backseat for the entire taxi ride to the airport. If the driver tried to speak to Carwyn or ask him anything during the trip, Carwyn was so out of it that he never heard a thing. Carwyn was jolted back to life by the cabbie slamming on the brakes—probably intentionally—as they arrived at the airport. He banged his head on the back of the seat in front of him.

"Fuck," he muttered to himself, and not because of his collision with the back of the seat. He had never gotten any cash to replenish his empty wallet. His mind raced. He felt embarrassed, but being in a new place and not having a good grasp on the culture or any grasp of the language, he felt more nervous than anything else. How would he possibly explain the situation? How would he remedy the situation? What would the gruff cabby do to him once he realized Carwyn had no money with which to pay the fare?

When the taxi stopped completely, Carwyn thought better of even attempting to mention his predicament while still inside the cab. Would he just grab his bag and run? Once out of the cab, Carwyn scanned the small crowd outside the airport for anyone who appeared like they could help him out of his predicament. In the meantime, the cabbie was retrieving Carwyn's backpack from the truck. Carwyn spotted an attendant that looked friendly enough and quickly approached.

"Do you speak English?"

"Da. You needzelp?"

"Yes, I need an ATM—a cash machine—to pay my taxi fare."

"Inside." And the man pointed vaguely inside and to the right somewhere.

"Can you explain to the driver?"

"Da, yes."

Carwyn darted inside and in the general direction the attendant had pointed. When he found the ATM, there was somebody already using the machine. Carwyn waited for what seemed like forever before the woman in front of him finally completed her transaction. As soon as she had retrieved her card, Carwyn practically knocked her over to get up to the machine and insert his debit card. *Thank God there's a language selection option.* Carwyn pressed the image of the Union Jack and then proceeded to select the withdrawal option. This particular bank-o-mat machine had quick-withdrawal options of 500, 1000, 1500, 2000, 3000, and 5000 rubles.

Carwyn, unsure of the conversion rate, selected the second-highest amount. *Surely three thousand will be enough.* After making his selection, the machine spent a long time thinking before it dispensed Carwyn's cash and then way too long to spit his card back out.

Carwyn half ran, half walked back toward the waiting cabbie. The only problem was that there was no cabbie waiting—which, incidentally, meant no backpack either. Stunned, Carwyn froze for an instant, as if standing there would make the cabbie return or make his backpack fall from the sky to his feet. Neither occurred. "Shit!"

Luckily Carwyn had his passport in his pocket and all his important documents crammed in his wallet. He didn't really have time to mourn the loss of a few clothes anyway. He had a plane to catch. He got his boarding pass, proceeded through security, and got to his gate just as they were about to shut the door. Barely having had any time to think from the moment he woke up in the cab until he had rushed through the airport to his gate, he had temporarily stopped noticing the physical effects of the previous night.

Once he was securely seated in his not-quite-big-enough-for-a-thirteen-hour-flight chair, the effects of the night before came rushing back. He thought he might be sick.

It seemed like days before the plane's engine got fully started, providing Carwyn with some much-needed air. It seemed like weeks before the plane finally got moving, left the earth, and took to the air.

Carwyn's flight was scheduled to touch down just before eleven o'clock at night. Carwyn hoped that he did not have the misfortune of being seated next to a big talker. He had been seated by big talkers in the past. He just couldn't take someone who wanted to blab for any great length of time over the course of a thirteen-hour flight.

He almost hoped that he still smelled like booze, which might discourage anyone from attempting to be overly friendly. Or, if he was lucky, his neighbor wouldn't be able to speak any English.

Just like every moment of waiting on this day so far, the time between takeoff and when the flight attendant finally started her beverage service down the aisle took ages. And it was like she was working in extreme slow motion. *Dear God, please hurry up*, thought Carwyn as she moved down the aisle and toward his seat. When she got to his seat, Carwyn asked for a ginger ale. It was like nectar from the fountain of youth (or something even better) when the cold, fizzy beverage hit his lips.

The only problem was that he was finished with his beverage by the time the flight attendant was only one row back. He desperately wanted another one. He'd probably have to wait until they served the in-flight meal. He hadn't really noticed it before, but he was starving.

After his not-horrible dinner, Carwyn was hoping that the in-flight movie options would provide him with at least one good choice to help pass the time in flight. It turned out that for the first time in his life, Carwyn would not need all that much help to pass the time. Carwyn was generally unable to sleep on planes, but he passed out about thirty minutes after having eaten his dinner.

When he woke about an hour from touchdown, it was as if the hangover he should already have experienced had been lying in wait. The pain of the pounding in Carwyn's head was exceeded only by the aching, stabbing, searing pain in his neck. His stomach really wasn't all that unsettled, but he definitely hoped there wouldn't be any turbulence before the plane began its descent. However, he would gladly have traded the remaining flight time for a little bit of turbulence. He really didn't know how he could take the confinement and the horrendous drone of the engine for even another five minutes.

Carwyn tried to go back to sleep for the remaining duration of the flight, but that was just not going to happen. As it turned out, the passenger beside him, who had previously been so joyfully untalkative, decided that now, at the very moment when Carwyn's head was pounding like never before, was the perfect time to have a chat.

"Blah, blah. Blah, blah, blah." That was basically all Carwyn heard, but he gave what must have been an appropriate response.

"Blah, blah, blah." This time, Carwyn had to try to nip any further conversation in the bud, so he grabbed the magazine from the seat back in front of him. He didn't plan to actually read anything.

"Blah?"

You've got to be kidding me, Carwyn thought. "Sir, I'm sorry. I don't mean to be rude, but I really don't think my in-flight meal is agreeing with me. I feel pretty sick, and I just want to sit here with my eyes closed for the rest of the flight." The passenger's one word response, "Okay," was music to Carwyn's ears. The music got even sweeter when the pilot's voice crackled over the PA system to announce that they would be making their final descent in about twenty minutes. Still, time moved slowly. When the plane began its descent, Carwyn instantly began to feel better. He didn't actually feel good, but he did feel better.

By the time Carwyn got home, it was after midnight. Although he had slept for hours on the plane, he still felt tired. *Thank God.* If he could sleep now for at least five or six hours, hopefully he could avoid jet lag, and just maybe his body would stop absolutely hating him.

— 33 —

EVERYBODY'S LUCK RUNS OUT some time, especially in a high-stakes place like Monte Carlo. Bret never could catch a lucky streak there. Even when he moved over to the Sun Casino and played at the American poker tables, Bret just couldn't catch the cards. Bret played his last hands in Monte Carlo, he experienced his last sunrise in Nice, and he never made it to Venice with Rebecca.

*   *   *   *

Carwyn woke as if from a trance to the sound of his cell phone ringing. He got up and checked the screen to see who it was before answering. *Rebecca?* He had her number in is phone, but he never called her, and she never called him.

"Hello."

"Carwyn?"

"Um, yeah."

"It's Rebecca."

"Right. What's going on?"

"Well, what are you doing right now?"

"Nothing. Laying in bed, why?"

"Well, I have some bad news."

Carwyn's heart skipped a beat, but he had no idea what to expect. "What kind of bad news?"

"It's about Bret."

Carwyn wondered if they had called off the wedding, but then why on earth would Rebecca be the one calling him? "What about Bret?"

"Well ..."

"Well?"

"Well, um I—I really just don't know any right way to say this, but Bret ... Bret is dead."

Silence. *Dead?* It didn't fully register with Carwyn at first, but then he understood the reason for the timbre of Rebecca's voice. It sounded as if she had recently been crying. And then the gravity of what she had just said registered with Carwyn. He didn't react all that strongly right away. He did not cry. Not then.

"What? What happened?"

"He was in an accident. Carwyn, it's awful. I'm sorry. He was—he got hit by a train. Two days ago. They say with the force of the impact, it would have been instant, that he wouldn't have felt any pain."

Likely as a defense mechanism against sadness and tears and loss, Carwyn, instead of any other emotional reaction, became angry.

"What the hell? Two days ago? And you're just now calling me?"

"Carwyn, I'm sorry, I just ..."

"You just what?"

"I just put off calling you, I just—it's just not a call that I wanted to make. I just didn't know how to tell you. I'm so sorry."

Carwyn instantly felt bad for his selfish anger. "Rebecca, I'm sorry. I guess my emotions just got the better of me. I should not have questioned you. This has just caught me very off guard, and I guess my brain hasn't quite figured out how to react. How are you?"

"Well, I mean, I'm ... doing okay."

But to Carwyn it seemed that she really wasn't. "Can I do anything?"

"No, I just need some time, I guess." Her voice started to quiver, and she said, "I have to—I should probably go. I'll call you with the funeral arrangements."

"Okay. If you need anything, let me know."

"I will, and the same goes for you."

"Sure."

"I'll talk to you later Carwyn, and I'm sorry."

"Me too."

And then the line went dead. Carwyn was left alone with his thoughts in the deafening silence. He had briefly experienced anger. Now he just felt numb. His best friend was dead. Gone. He pulled the covers up over his head. He just wanted to go back to sleep. Sleep would block things out. He still had not fully registered Rebecca's call, still had not fully felt the loss, felt the emptiness and sadness. Those feelings would come later. He still had not cried. The tears would come later too.

Part 3

(AFTER EUROPE
AND CLOSER TO NOW)

34

THE BUSINESSMAN HAD PICKED out his next negotiating chip. He had hired four people to help him complete the transaction. Too many cohorts complicated and confused matters, impeding progress—not to mention cutting into profit. All four men that had been hired would assist in picking up the collateral and keeping her captive until the final transaction took place. After that, they would never all work together at the same time again. There was still much preparation and work to be done, but once the initial selection was made, everything else tended to fall into place quite nicely. The businessman was getting excited.

*   *   *   *

Lately—well, for a few months now—nothing seemed to be going his way. Carwyn's mother, according to Carwyn's memory, had not actively supported many of his varying interests as a child, whether it had been his desire to be an actor, or a writer, or especially when he thought about pursuing a degree in philosophy.

In retrospect, he was actually grateful for that one. He already overthought everything. Overthinking only led to worrying, and worrying never really got anybody anywhere. *There is no meaning, no purpose.* He wished he liked gin. He wished he had asked Megan Ambrose out in sixth grade.

Paradoxically enough, it was his own mother now who, after watching *Pursuit of Happyness* for the first time, thought that all could be solved, that Carwyn could get just the job he had always wanted—the perfect job to enrich his mind, heart, and soul (and wallet)—if only he would walk right up to just the right person and solve a Rubik's Cube in record time. Well, he had already had the perfect job, hadn't he? And he had taken a dump right on it. He wished he had learned how to play an instrument. *Maybe I will buy a fucking Rubik's Cube.*

Carwyn felt frustrated, apathetic, angry, and on edge all at the same time. He felt like he could or would do anything, like he didn't even know what he might do from one day or even one minute to the next. It was as if he was stalking a spark, hunting for something of consequence to happen in his life, an excuse to do something of consequence. He needed to break through the apathy and let the anger out by doing something heart-stirring, something heart-stopping.

*   *   *   *

It had been some months since Carwyn returned from Europe without Bret. Bret, his best friend, whom he could no longer talk too. Bret, at whose wedding he would never make a funny, slightly embarrassing and inappropriate but ultimately heartfelt toast. He had completed a draft of the speech, typed it up on his computer, and printed it out. He hadn't included all the embarrassing anecdotes he likely would have included in the real version, but that didn't really matter now. He was never going to give the speech or toast or whatever the fuck it was.

Carwyn had folded and folded the printout into a little square and put it in the back of a drawer. He had made sure to keep it from getting lost when he moved to Montpelier, Vermont from Bristol, Connecticut. He had unfolded it and read it aloud to himself a time or two over the past several months:

> On behalf of Bret and Rebecca, please allow me to thank all of you: friends, family, all you other people who have ventured from both near and far to share this remarkably special day. I, for one, feel honored to be here. But enough with the pleasantries. No one individual is perfect, and my friend Bret is certainly no exception, although he was on the top of the dean's list in college, on top of a lot of the dean's things, actually. Despite Bret's imperfections (and let me tell you, they are many), when two individuals are drawn together, be it by accident, fate, serendipity, luck, hard work, stalking, etcetera, it can create a spark of perfection through the strength of those individuals' love for each other. Love is such a short, simple word, and yet it

is a remarkably poignant and powerful emotion. It can be an infinitely confusing and abstract concept representing with just four letters, the grandest of thoughts, feelings, and experiences. Love manifests itself in a wide variety of ways, but love itself is never all that simple. All you need to do is turn on the radio or change the TV channel to Lifetime to understand that. But seriously, I think the philosopher Friedrich Nietzsche may have said it best when he said, "There is always some madness in love. But there is also always some reason in madness." Of course, when Nietzsche said it, it may just have been the syphilis talking. Well, whatever the reason that Bret and Rebecca found each other, and whatever the reason they have fallen for each other, be it syphilis or sweet serendipity, I sincerely hope that the spark of their love ignites a flame to warm their hearts and souls, to guide them through the inevitable dark times, and to solder their independent spirits together indefinitely, not as one being or one life, for a marriage should not stifle the individuality of those entering into it, but together, as two complementary and indispensable pieces of one beautiful journey. Bret, you are my best friend, and I wish you all the happiness you can possible wring out of this life. And Rebecca, I'm more than happy to call you my best-friend-in-law. You make Bret a better man, and I am sure that you would agree that he has brought out the best in you. May you both continue to bring out the best in each other and continue to make each other better versions of yourselves. I truly do love you both. So here is to love, and yes, also to madness. But most importantly, to Bret and Rebecca's journey and to their continuing pursuit of perfection.

Sometimes Carwyn wondered if he had been writing about Bret and Rebecca or about what he himself was missing and needing.

*   *   *   *

Not that it made any damn difference now, but in a moment of motivation about a month after he had returned from Europe, Carwyn had actually applied for, been offered, and accepted a position as a writer with ESPN. He had picked himself up and moved to Bristol, Connecticut. He had only been working for a few weeks when he had his climbing accident.

He tore the ACL and MCL in his right knee. He wrecked his meniscus. He broke his right foot and his left wrist. He damn near killed himself. Well, his wrist and foot ended up healing just fine in about eight weeks, but his knee never did. He started popping shellfish-free glucosamine like it was going out of style, like it was crack, just hoping, and even praying, that, like some magic pill from *The Matrix* or *Alice in Wonderland*, it would miraculously fix his knee. It didn't. `He wished he wasn't allergic to shellfish.`

It was several weeks after Carwyn's accident that Vivian stopped calling and e-mailing. There was no warning, no explanation, nothing. Just. *Nothing.* She even blocked him on Facebook. After the first week without hearing from her, Carwyn called and e-mailed Vivian a few times. Then he called her another time or two, followed by one final e-mail about six or seven weeks after her last communication. His worry turned to fear, which turned briefly to anger, which turned to sadness, which, when compounded by his knee and other external factors (losing his job, having no money, Bret's death, no friends in Montpelier), festered to melancholy and eventually to something akin to diagnosable depression.

The final straw came when, after he got fired, he had to move in with his mother, who had moved to Montpelier, Vermont. Carwyn didn't know a single person other than his mother in Montpelier. His sister had moved to California, and his brother was still in college in Ohio. Montpelier was certainly not a thriving metropolis. `He wished he spoke a foreign language (or two) fluently.`

It was while feeling trapped in quite possibly the United States' most boring state capital that Carwyn's deepening depression became envenomed, turning to the undirected anger that had him on edge. It was an emotional state Carwyn had never really experienced and could not even fully explain. He was numb, apathetic, but at the same time filled with a nondescript bitterness.

On some level, he probably needed the bitterness and anger to help him feel like he actually existed. Maybe without the anger he would have felt nothing at all. And maybe, feeling nothing, he would have faded into the background of existence or simply eroded into nonexistence like some sad, agoraphobic octogenarian whose cats had all run away or like New Hampshire's Old Man of the Mountain.

Whatever the reason for his anger, more and more often Carwyn noticed his inner Tyler Durden starting to emerge—some subconscious part of himself that was in need of some reaction, any sort of reaction.

— 35 —

"HEY THERE, SUNSHINE," SAID Steven Dorchester, the self-righteous assistant manager at Carwyn's new, crappy place of employment, Peak Performance. Dorchester (called Dorkchester behind his back by many Peak Performance employees) looked liked he'd never even been outside, let alone taken part in any outdoor athletic or recreational activities. Yet he was always breathing down Carwyn's neck to sell more gear.

Carwyn almost put his entire third paycheck toward a plane ticket to Amsterdam to go and seek out Vivian. Then he thought better of it. And then he overanalyzed his better judgment: *As many people as one might see and meet and interact with in one's lifetime, that grand total is only an infinitesimal portion of the billions of people roaming this earth (and those who lived and died before us, whose roaming days have come to an end). So, amid the happenstance, serendipity, and geochronological coincidentalism of any one human life crossing paths with another, when such an intersection results in the occurrence of a singular, prodigiously wondrous and electromagnetic eventuality, perhaps the seemingly serendipitous intersection should not be viewed as a mere accident of time and space but more as a fortuity to be appreciated and nurtured (not that any particular fatelike or magical quality need be specifically attributed to the event). Maybe I should have better nurtured the product of my fortuitously meeting Vivian.* Carwyn regretted—no, he *hated* his better judgment. *I am a coward.*

What Carwyn wanted more than anything was to see Vivian again. He wanted to see her one-of-a-kind smile, to smell the tantalizing shampoo in her hair, to feel the touch of her hand, to taste her kiss, to hear her laugh. Since the first moment he had met Vivian, not a single day had gone by in which Carwyn had not thought about her at least once.

36

THAT EVENING ON THE way home from work after a full day of putting up with Dorchester, Carwyn's mood was, as typical, on edge. He was definitely feeling more than just a little surly. Vivian. Knee. Job. No money. No friends. Bret being gone. Living with his mother. Fucking Dorchester.

About five or six minutes from home, a BMW SUV attempted to cut Carwyn off. Carwyn was not in the mood, however, and did not give way even an inch to the impatient SUV. In fact, Carwyn sped up out of principle (what principle, Carwyn did not know). Principle got him a dent in his car and a pissed off motorist.

Carwyn could see the driver of the SUV vigorously motioning for Carwyn to pull off the road, presumably to exchange insurance information. Carwyn had recently let his car insurance lapse, so his first impulse was to ignore the man and continue home. For some reason, however, Carwyn found himself following the SUV and pulling into a more-or-less empty parking lot. Although he probably could have avoided the accident, Carwyn felt that it wasn't his fault. He was feeling empowered by a little righteous indignation.

Carwyn put his car in park but didn't turn off the engine. He really didn't know what he was going to say to the man in the SUV. He got out of his car, not sure what to expect.

As it turned out, Carwyn didn't have to say much at all. The other driver was ready to speak enough for both of them. As the other driver got out of his much more expensive vehicle, he was already swearing. He approached Carwyn as if he was going to hit him, but Carwyn got the sense that this dog's bite was worse than his bark.

"You stupid little shit, who the fuck do you think you are?"

No response from Carwyn.

"Did you hear me, retard?"

Retard? Carwyn still didn't feel like he owed this man any response, so he remained silent.

"You know you're gonna pay for my damage, right? My car is worth more than you and everything you own."

Then the man got up in Carwyn's face and demanded, "Give me your contact information."

Carwyn thought about punching the guy right in the mouth, but despite the anger that had taken root within him recently, he was not a violent person. But this guy was being a pretentious jackass.

Carwyn slapped him hard right across the face. The man was stunned and, for the first time since he had stepped out of his vehicle, silent. Carwyn still didn't say a word. He just got back into his car and drove off.

Adrenaline was pumping through Carwyn's body by the time he pulled out of the parking lot, his fight-or-flight response kicking in after he had already done a little bit of both. He was so amped up that he almost hit another car before he had made it a mile. As the adrenaline rush subsided, Carwyn reflected on his actions. *What the hell?*

He felt guilty, justified, and satisfied all at the same time. Carwyn had never slapped anyone in the face before. He had been in one or two minor scraps before, but he had never been the one either to start or to finish things. That just wasn't his nature. *But that guy did kind of deserve it.*

At home, with the engine off, Carwyn remained in his car and listed to the end of "Fool in the Rain" by Zeppelin. Carwyn contemplated the fact that there are few more sacred spaces for a man than the driver seat of his own car with a good song turned up on the radio. The right song can have one hell of an impact. "Fool in the Rain" was one of Carwyn's favorite classic rock songs. It was definitely his favorite Zeppelin song. While the song helped Carwyn forget the asshole in the SUV, he also felt that the song was somehow a musical metaphor for his life. Maybe he was just a fool waiting on the wrong block.

— 37 —

EXCEPT FOR THE SUV asshole, it had been a day like any other: work, boredom, frustration, anger. Just a day. It was a day like months of days before—until Carwyn got out of his car, went inside and down to his basement bedroom, turned on his laptop, and checked his e-mail. There were five e-mails. Just five. Some people got that many in an hour (or less). Carwyn got five all day, and four were more or less spam. The fifth was certainly *not* junk. He recognized the address right away: BelViv510.

Science regressed and the experimentation of Louis Pasteur was instantly debunked as an epic biological fraud, as right then and there a family of butterflies spontaneously generated in Carwyn's stomach. He didn't even know what he was feeling. If a crazed gunman had burst into Carwyn's room at that exact moment, held a gun to Carwyn's head, and demanded that he describe his precise emotional state, it would have likely been curtains for poor Carwyn.

His mind was a torrent. He probably looked at Vivian's e-mail address (there was no subject line) for a full two minutes before he clicked to open the e-mail.

Carwyn:

First, I want to say that I am sorry that I haven't returned any of your calls or e-mails for so long, for too long. I started seeing someone, just briefly, (I guess I am more needy than I want to believe), and I didn't know how to break that to you. I guess I was afraid of what I might lose, what I might be giving up. But not a single day has gone by that I haven't thought about you. I think you took a small piece of my soul/sole :) with you when you left Amsterdam. I know that it probably sounds stupid and corny and selfish to tell you that after all this time, but you are the greatest thing that I ever lucked into. I guess I should also say that I am not seeing that guy anymore. He was just another not-you. Not that I am expecting anything by telling you that. Hoping? Maybe. Probably ... definitely.

Anyway, what I am writing you about is my dad. He is sick. My mom wants me to come home. I thought maybe you could pick me up at the airport and drive with me to Ottawa. Maybe in a twisted way it's a sign or something. Not that I even really believe in such things. Of course I would pay for gas and food.

I miss you so much, and it would mean a lot to me to see you and spend some time with you. I know this is out of the blue after so long, and I know you don't owe me anything at all, but I want to see you even more than I care to admit to myself. I can only hope that you may want to see me too.

I hope you don't hate me or resent me (or worse, not care anymore at all) for not calling or writing for so long. I was scared. I was stupid. I was childish. I was selfish.

So I know this is very last minute, but I am flying into Logan Airport, and I arrive next week on the 27th at 4:08 p.m.

Please e-mail me back and let me know if you will be able (and willing) to pick me up. I sure hope you will.

Yours,
Vivian.

Yours? Carwyn felt like he was trapped in a bad movie. *Yours?* His eyes welled up, and a couple of tears actually fell from each eye. *Yours?*

His instant, almost reflexive emotional response was a kind of happiness. But that happiness was promptly followed (though not overtaken) by disconsolateness. Vivian had been seeing somebody else. *Seeing? What does that mean? Hanging out with? Sleeping with? Briefly? How long is briefly?* His disconsolateness was then joined by a sort of embarrassment. He did not experience any anger, and Carwyn wondered whether the absence of that emotion was a good thing or whether no anger meant that he didn't really care all that much after all.

He felt fear and uncertainty, and then all the positive feelings he felt made him feel foolish. And then he felt foolish for feeling foolish. *Yours?*

After all the time he had been waiting for her (if he was being honest with himself, he really had been waiting for her), now that the prospect of seeing her again hung in the air, contingent only upon an affirmative response from him, Carwyn had some potent misgivings. *If she was willing to treat me the way she treated me, is she really worth it?* Would some lack of forgiveness always linger, or worse, mutate into bitterness? He wanted her, but *should* he want to want her? And what was worse, even though he had never worried about Vivian's clientele, Carwyn was now unable to stop picturing her with some mystery guy.

Carwyn realized that he had no claim to Vivian, that she owed him nothing. But he wanted her to want to owe him more than she'd given. He knew no other girl like Vivian had ever drawn or would ever draw a breath on this earth. She was the only one that could be *the* one—not that everybody was fortunate enough to actually end up with the one, and sometimes ironically enough, *the* one just does not work out.

Carwyn could almost hear U2's "With or Without You" playing in his head. He had always kind of thought that song was a little melodramatic and far-fetched, but now …

The past several months Carwyn really hadn't been able to live without Vivian, but after she had simply chosen to disregard his existence (as if he had never been of any real importance in her life), he was unsure that he could ever really, truly live *with* her. Carwyn

143

figured that erring on the side of with was better than erring on the side of without. *WWBD? What Would Bono Do?*

Carwyn laughed a weird, nervous-excited laugh. Maybe he actually *needed* Vivian. It was like those first butterflies in his stomach had migrated to his brain. He was a giant ball of tumultuous, overthinking, oxymoronic paradoxicality. *Yours? Yours.* Even with his monsoon of mixed emotions, Carwyn couldn't fight off a smile.

Carwyn looked down to see his fingers typing. His response simply read, "I'll see you on the 27th." He did not hit the send button. He had to think about it. No, he did *not* have to think about it. He knew the answer; he just had to find the right words. Carwyn's fingers tap, tap, tapped across his keyboard, and he amended his message to read:

> Vivian,
>
> I am sorry to hear about your dad. Do you know what is wrong with him? I am sure he will be okay.
>
> And it is good to hear from you. I can pick you up on the 27th, but you don't need to worry about gas and food. Well, maybe some gas :)
>
> See you soon,
> Carwyn

He didn't like the sound of "what is wrong with him," but he couldn't think of any better choice of words to get that point across, and he felt that he had to ask.

The next day at work was pretty uneventful, but Carwyn's anger and frustration both seemed to have dissipated. Vivian's impending visit was like two fingers of a good scotch, neat, for his consciousness and his soul. It warmed him up and took the edge off. Carwyn decided to take a week off from work, starting the day of Vivian's arrival.

— 38 —

Vivian's flight into Logan was on time (so declared the handy airport monitors), and Carwyn anxiously awaited her arrival. Carwyn had arrived at the airport much too early, and he had mulled around doing nothing at all, trying to pass the time until Vivian's plane landed. He was not about to simply pick her up at the curb. He walked through about half the stores in the airport. He contemplated buying some sort of welcoming gift, but he didn't know what to get, and it would have been cheesy anyway. By 3:45 p.m., Carwyn was planted by the exit from terminal E.

Passengers trickled out the exit. About fifteen minutes after Carwyn had stationed himself there, the slow trickle of passengers turned into a steady flow. Carwyn assumed Vivian's plane must have landed. Carwyn stood off to the side, butterflies all aflutter, waiting for Vivian to come walking out the exit. The passengers continued to stream out. Carwyn waited. It was hardly that long at all, but it seemed like half an eternity.

The steady flow of passengers exiting the causeway gradually dwindled back to a trickle and then to infrequent drops. Then the stream stopped. Just a couple minutes later, more people started coming through the exit. No Vivian. Carwyn waited through four or five distinctive waxings and wanings. No Vivian.

Carwyn saw hundreds of passengers with distinctive emotions expressed on their faces and different clothing adorning their bodies. Amongst the passengers Carwyn observed, there were surely those who were returning home after being gone for too long—or not long enough. There were passengers who were arriving to seal, negotiate, or renegotiate some business deal—or to begin a vacation. There were perhaps some who were just passing through on their way to another distant part of the country or the world. But all of the passengers had at least one thing in common. They were all *not* Vivian.

Still Carwyn waited. He scanned the groups of recently exited passengers heading off to their various destinations to make sure he hadn't missed her. He wouldn't have missed her; who was he kidding? He wasn't quite sure what to do. He waited another minute or two more. No Vivian.

Carwyn approached an attendant.

"Ma'am?"

"Yes, sir?"

"Hi. Um, I was waiting on a passenger flying in from Amsterdam, but I don't think she got off the plane. I never saw her. Well, I know she didn't get off the plane. I wouldn't have missed her. I'm kind of worried. She was flying in on Aer Lingus."

"Well, someone might be able to check to see if she boarded the plane in Amsterdam in the first place, but that's about all I can suggest. If she did board in Amsterdam, it's possible she could have missed a connecting flight."

The attendant directed Carwyn to an Aer Lingus desk. The Aer Lingus employee apologized but informed Carwyn that for security reasons the airline could not divulge whether any specific passenger was on or had been on any specific flight.

"If you have her phone number, you might try calling her directly."

"Right. Thank you." Carwyn felt like an idiot for not already thinking of something so simple himself.

"My pleasure, sir. Can I help you with anything else?"

"No. Thank you."

Carwyn dejectedly made his way toward the exit. *I guess she changed her mind and decided she didn't want to come*, he thought. He decided to give Vivian a call. There was no answer. Not in any sort of mood to care whether anyone overheard him talking to himself, Carwyn muttered, "I guess that figures. If she bailed on her flight, she sure isn't gonna answer her phone."

Just as Carwyn put his phone back into his pocket, it rang. A moment of hope. He answered his phone without looking to see who the incoming call was from.

"Hello?"

A European accent greeted him. "Mr. Hillis?" It definitely was *not* Vivian.

Hope dashed, Carwyn replied, "That's me. Can I help you?"

"I'm a friend of a friend."

"And what friend is that?"

"Well, that will become clear momentarily. Are you somewhere you can sit down and pay very close attention to what I have to tell you?"

"Do you want something?"

"Well, I am a businessman, Mr. Hillis, and I have a proposition for you."

"What kind of proposition? What the hell are you talking about?"

"Well, let's just say it has the potential to be a very lucrative venture."

"Is this some kind of a joke?

"It is no joke, Mr. Hillis. I told you I have a proposition, and I think you are going to want to hear me out."

Carwyn, already upset and frustrated by Vivian's no-show, was really starting to lose his patience. "Well, what the shit do you want?"

"Best not to get agitated, Mr. Hillis, and really, there is no need to use profane language."

"Okay, man, whoever you are, I'm hanging up on you."

"I would not do that if I where you, Mr. Hilli—"

Carwyn ended the call. He reinitiated his doleful march to the airport exit. Just as he got to the door, his phone rang. Again without checking the ID, Carwyn answered his phone.

"Hello."

It was the same voice on the line, but this time it seemed devoid of any empathy or redeeming human influence. It was cold, almost soulless. The tone and timbre of the man's voice stopped Carwyn in his tracks.

"Carwyn, do not hang up the phone this time or you will come to deeply regret it."

The man's voice sent a chill through Carwyn's body. He couldn't respond.

"Mr. Hillis, are you there?" It was the cordial, pleasantly businesslike voice again. The distinction was absolutely subtle, and that subtlety made it all the more unnerving.

"I'm here."

"Good. Now I am going to need you to listen to me very carefully.

Can you do that? I think you should go to someplace quiet and private so you can pay full attention to what I have to say."

"Well, I'm almost to my car. Can you wait just a minute?"

"I can."

Carwyn hastily completed the walk to his car. He got in and shut the door but didn't start the engine. He sat in the dim light and placed the phone back to his ear. "Okay."

"So, Mr. Hillis, you wanted to know who our mutual friend is, correct?"

"Yes."

"She is quite the pretty young lady."

It hadn't yet clicked for Carwyn, and he asked, "Who are you talking about?"

"What, so quick to forget your beautiful Canadian friend?" It clicked then, almost like a loaded magazine being slotted into a gun with a shaky finger at the trigger.

"Vivian?"

"There you go, Mr. Hillis. Now you are catching up and catching on. You might make for a good business partner after all."

"But what are you calling about? I don't know what you're talking about. I don't even know your name."

"My name is not important right now, Mr. Hillis. What is important is the kind of businessman I am and the kind of businessman you are capable of being. Do you remember I told you I was a businessman, Mr. Hillis?"

"I remember, Mr. Not Important."

"That is very clever, Mr. Hillis, but cleverness will get you nowhere. Do you remember I said that I have a proposition for you?"

"Yes."

"Well, I have something you want, and you have the money to obtain it. Supply and demand, Mr. Hillis. Supply and demand."

"You aren't making any sense."

The soulless voice returned. "No, you are not paying close enough attention, Carwyn."

"What is your damn proposition?"

"Vivian's life is in your hands. Currently, I have her. I am in control. She is safe—for now. However, I am not against using every single orifice of her body for my own personal satisfaction and then allowing each and every one of my business associates to do the exact same thing … and Mr. Hillis, they are not all as considerate and professional as I am, though I expect they would do nothing to her she has not already been paid to do. However, when we are done with her, we will simply dispose of her. And by dispose, Mr. Hillis, what I mean is shoot her in the head, dismember her, and mail her teeth and ears to you. But of course, like I said before, I am a businessman. I am not unreasonable. I am willing to offer you a one-of-a-kind business opportunity. For the small investment of only eight hundred thousand euros, what is mine will become yours. Instead of just the teeth and ears, you can have the whole pretty thing. Even all the parts you have already paid for."

When the man on the other end of the line spoke those words, his voice did not change back into that cold soulless voice that had so easily captured Carwyn's attention. He spoke with the same calm, measured, matter-of-fact tone as he had during the first call. And that smooth directness—as if he really was talking about some legitimate business venture—made the words he spoke all the more sinister. They hung in the air like a poisonous haze: *every single orifice; shoot her in the head; dismember.*

But Carwyn did not respond. He was in a state of shock. He had no idea what to say. What do you say in response to something that cold, that violent, that raw and inhuman? Time seemed frozen for an instant. The silence loomed like a deadly accurate sniper camouflaged and waiting for just the right change in the wind to take out his mark. Then the man on the other end broke the silence.

"Are you still there, Mr. Hillis?

It took a moment more for Carwyn to answer. The schoolboy butterflies that had been playfully flittering about in his stomach for hours seemed to become anxious themselves and accelerate their flight. It was as if the butterflies had collectively amassed enough strength to dislodge Carwyn's heart from behind the protective confines of his sternum and raise it up into his throat. Carwyn found it hard to breathe. He found it difficult to swallow, let alone to speak. Finally the words "I'm here" fumbled from his lips.

"Good. Now, I need you to remain calm and focused. Are you calm, Mr. Hillis?"

"No, not really. I mean, I guess, as much as I can be."

"That will have to suffice for now. Are you focused?"

"As much as I can be."

"Well, that will do for the time being. Now, as I am a shrewd businessman, I realize that such a risky business venture might require some deliberation on your part, so I am going to give you two days to think about my offer, and then I am going to call back for your answer. If you decide to go forward with the venture, I will give you further details and instructions at that time. If my proposition does not seem like a venture that you would be interested in, just remember, I will kill the whore ... but only after she has suffered greatly. Two days."

"Wait, how—" said Carwyn, but the line went dead. In the eerie silence, there seemed to be an almost supernatural glow from the lights of the parking garage. In the dim light and the quiet, Carwyn was scared and on edge, but the situation still had not fully registered. He sat motionless in his car.

Off in a remote corner of the parking garage, a door slammed. Carwyn jumped. The sudden noise startled him out of his fearful trance. As if someone had pulled the trigger of that loaded gun in his mind, all the fear, anxiety, shock, anger, and confusion shot to the forefront of his consciousness.

Carwyn wiped his face. He looked up into his rearview mirror, more to look at himself and examine how the raw emotions had affected his appearance than out of apprehension or fear or any sort of vigilance. He was alone in the garage.

Almost reflexively, Carwyn turned his key in the ignition. Even the grumbling to life of his own car made him jump. He sat with his engine idling for several minutes before he finally reversed out of his parking spot and began his unpleasant drive home.

As if the fitful butterflies, weakened by Carwyn's own devitalization, could no longer bear the weight of his heart, it seemed to drop back into place with a thud. Carwyn's heart, now safely nestled back in his ribcage, was still pounding. It felt as if his ribcage was actually vibrating. He tried to ignore it and concentrate on the road, but he just couldn't seem to focus on anything. He didn't know what to do, what to think, what to feel. He just drove. Slowly, the thudding Carwyn could feel both in his chest and his temples began to taper off.

39

CARWYN DIDN'T KNOW HOW long he had sat in his car before leaving the airport or how long he had been driving, but as he continued to drive he noticed that all traces of light had left the sky. He looked at the clock in his car. It was almost ten o'clock. The next thing he noticed was the orange gas light on his dashboard. He knew from experience that his car always had about twenty more miles left went it got to empty, but he had no idea how long it had been there. If he had really been driving for over three hours, he might be dangerously close to an actual empty tank.

When he looked up to check for a gas station, he saw a sign indicating that Burlington, Vermont was ten miles away. In his state of shock, he had driven almost thirty miles out of the way.

After he filled up, Carwyn got back in his car, but he didn't start it up. He sat there for a while thinking about the nightmarish phone call. But he wasn't really thinking. He was tired, and thoughts just kept darting around in his head. None of his thoughts stayed in place long enough for his consciousness to get a firm grip on them and consider them fully.

It was as if he was a practiced Buddhist monk allowing thoughts to pass through his mind, not holding on to them, not letting anything consume him, free of worry. But he was *not* free of worry—quite the opposite. Worry was working its way through his entire being. His mind and body just seemed to be too tired to actively experience it.

Just as he was about to turn his key in the ignition, a funny thing happened. Inexplicably, he began wondering if the depraved business venture (as the faceless, nameless, soulless voice—Mr. Not Important— had dubbed it) was some kind of twisted joke on Vivian's part, some cruel way of conveying the message that she was no longer interested in having anything to do with him.

It was a sick and cynical thought, but out of a profound need for it to be true more than from any truly rational acceptance of its veracity, Carwyn began to believe in his twistedly optimistic explanation. It was better for Vivian to be cold and cruel and safe than for her to be at the mercy of Mr. Not Important. Carwyn continued to contemplate his theory as he started his car, and by the time he had merged onto 89 South, his self-brainwashing was complete. He had convinced himself in much the same way that a sick person can convince himself or herself that nothing is really wrong.

The night was starless and dark. Carwyn almost wished he could go into another fugue state and simply end up at home without knowing how he had gotten there. As he made his way home, he struggled to stay awake. Three or four times during his journey, the cacophony of his tires on the highway rumble strip roused him from microsleep. Each time, his heart rate accelerated. His drive home took only about thirty-five minutes, but it seemed like hours.

When he got back to his mom's house, he marched, trance-like, straight down to his room, collapsed on his bed, and without even taking off his shoes, he was out cold in less than five minutes.

When Carwyn woke the next morning, he was highly disoriented. As the events of the night before slowly surfaced in his consciousness, the fear, anger, and sadness he had experienced were all displaced by a new apathy. It was now Thursday night, and he had taken a week off from work expecting to spend the time with Vivian. Now that she had cruelly stood him up, he didn't know what to do with himself. He still didn't really know anybody in Montpelier well enough to call them up to do anything. After that stupid call from one of Vivian's stupid friends, he might normally have called Bret, but that was no longer an option.

Carwyn thought briefly about calling Rebecca but figured that would have been far too awkward. He decided he'd just order a pizza, open a bottle of wine, and watch a movie—a good action or comedy movie he could get lost in. He went through his movie cabinet, but nothing jumped out at him, so he called in his order for a large pepperoni and mushroom pizza and ventured out to his car.

At the video store, he meandered through the aisles and picked out both a comedy and an action flick. It had started to drizzle lightly while he was in the video store, but he hardly noticed it.

Part 4

(ALMOST NOW)

40

THE TWO DAYS ALLOTTED by Mr. Not Important passed without Carwyn really even noticing. He had convinced himself that the situation was not real, that the reality was much less brutal (although probably equally as bleak and maybe even suicide-grade depressing—not that Carwyn would ever have taken his own life). It was about seven in the evening, and Carwyn was watching ESPN, his apathy smoldering into self-loathing, when his phone rang. The phone number showed up on his screen as a series of zeros. Carwyn almost didn't answer, but then something inside him compelled him to take the call.

"Hello?"

"Mr. Hillis, how are you today?"

"Look, man, whoever you are, you can tell Vivian that her sense of humor sucks."

"Sense of humor? Oh, you still are not taking me seriously—what a shame. I can tell you Ms. Belanger is *not* in a joking mood." Then he hung up. A few minutes later, Carwyn received a text message alert. When he went to open the message, he noticed that it was a multimedia message. The screen was black, but after about a second, he heard that now all-too-familiar European accent declare, "I wish you had taken me more seriously. It would have saved Ms. Belanger a lot of pain and suffering."

Then a video began to play: Vivian, naked, bound to a chair with her arms behind her back and a gag in her mouth. A man wearing a black ski mask came into view. First he released her arms. Then, from one of his pockets, he produced a small rectangular razor blade and moved down between Vivian's legs. Then the accented voice spoke again: "As we intend only to make sure that you take us seriously and not to permanently disfigure Ms. Belanger in any conspicuous way, we are going to utilize the underside of her arm, where no one will ever be able to see any marks or scars."

Vivian's eyes grew wide. Her fear looked real. The man in the black ski mask lifted one of her arms. Then, with depraved nonchalance, he took the small razor blade to her arm and sliced into her flesh, straight down the underside of her arm, leaving a thin, scarlet trail of blood in the blade's wake.

Through her gag, Vivian let out a muffled but nonetheless piercing scream—a *real* scream. The voice with the European accent said, "I am going to give you some time to let this sink in. I will call you back in one hour." The video zoomed in on Vivian's arm, but he could not watch, could not look. He quickly stopped the video and then dropped his phone, almost as if it was on fire or covered in acid. Carwyn could not see his own face, but he could almost feel the color leaving his skin. He ran to the bathroom to splash some water on his face but found that when he got there, it was for another reason. Carwyn quickly lifted the toilet seat and vomited into the porcelain bowl. He felt light-headed. He felt fear. For the first time in his life, he felt truly, helplessly, almost debilitatingly—and exhilaratingly—afraid.

Time stopped. Time moved in fast forward. The world faded to black. The world exploded in gaudy, tainted colors. The bathroom seemed to be spinning. The bathroom seemed deathly still and quiet. Carwyn's blood ran cold. Carwyn's blood ran hot. And then he was angry.

He was angry at himself for not believing the man in the first place. He thought to himself that what had just happened to Vivian was his fault. He felt nauseous again. He retched, but nothing came up. Carwyn gazed into the bathroom mirror, attempting to peer through his flesh and muscle and bone to see if he could discern whether he had the inner strength to cope with the current situation. But of course he couldn't see through his flesh or see into himself; and the man in the mirror had no more answers than he did. All Carwyn could do was wait.

41

AT ABOUT A QUARTER after eight, Carwyn's phone rang. He had been sitting in silence with his phone securely in his right hand. The ringing phone jolted him. Carwyn answered immediately, his fear manifesting itself in the form of anger and bravado. "You motherfucker, if you touch Vivian again, I swear, I will—" Click. The man on the other end had hung up before Carwyn could finish his empty threat. *What the?*

Carwyn was a wreck. He had no idea what to do. There was a class five hurricane ragging in his skull. Five minutes later, another text message came in—another video message. This time Vivian's captor warned Carwyn, "You must remain calm and polite, Mr. Hillis. Nothing will be accomplished through the use of harsh words or tones. You must remember that while I am in charge, Ms. Belanger's life is in your hands. If I am forced to terminate another call, I will assume that you simply do not care about Ms. Belanger's physical appearance or her overall well-being, and things will get very messy. Watch this new video we have prepared for you, and I will call you in fifteen minutes."

Carwyn could not bring himself to watch the video, so he just fidgeted nervously with his phone. The fifteen minutes he waited before his phone finally rang again seemed to take even longer than the hour he had waited previously. Time had no meaning. When Carwyn answered, he simply said, "Hello?"

"Much better, Mr. Hillis, much more friendly and polite. You sound much more like someone I can see myself doing business with."

"Well, just tell me what I have to do."

"I like your new attitude. It is simple: all you have to do is deliver to me eight hundred thousand euros."

"Eight hundred thousand euros? That's gotta be, what, about a million dollars?"

"A little more than that, I believe, Mr. Hillis. Do we have a deal?"

"I don't have any way to get my hands on that kind of money."

"Do not be modest, Mr. Hillis, or dishonest. I know you can make this transaction."

"But I can't. I really cannot get that kind of money."

"Well, that would be a very real shame for Ms. Belanger. If you are unable to get us the money, she will have to be gang-raped, murdered, and disposed of. Perhaps you should discuss things with Mr. or Mrs. Hightower."

Mr. or Mrs. Hightower? What the fuck is this fucking psycho talking about? How the fuck does he know anything about Bret? But Carwyn, who could now add confusion to his ever growing list of concurrent emotions, a list which already included fear, frustration, anger, and so forth, didn't want to leave Mr. Not Important hanging too long, and he wasn't going to have a conversation about Bret or inform Mr. Not Important that Bret was dead.

"Okay, okay. I—I will try to get the money, but I have no idea how to get it to you."

"Well, I hope you do more than just try, Mr. Hillis, and you will deliver the money to me in person, of course. Many people like to handle such business transactions electronically, but I like the face-to-face approach. I like to shake hands with my business partners and look them in the eyes. Call me old-fashioned."

Carwyn felt the urge to respond with some sort of sarcastic or aggressive retort, but his fear of what might happen to Vivian kept him calm. Well, it didn't really keep him calm; it just gave him reason to *act* calm.

"But where am I going to be taking the money?"

"How about Nürnberg, Germany. Does that work for you?"

"Well, uh, I guess it has to, doesn't it?"

"You are a wise man, Mr. Hillis, a fast learner. I am glad that I decided to do business with you."

"So where specifically am I going to be bringing the money?"

"I will text you an address. Now, do you think you are going to be able to get the money and get to Nürnberg any sooner than Tuesday, or are you going to need all of the time we have allowed?"

"That's only four days from now. I think I will need all of the time."

"Well, Tuesday it is then."

"And when you get the money, you will release Vivian?"

"It is as simple as that, Mr. Hillis. I have made these types of deals before, and I always honor my word if the money is on time. And one very important thing: you cannot tell anyone about our deal. Telling anyone about our deal would make things much worse for Ms. Belanger than if you did absolutely nothing at all. Do you understand?"

"Yes, I do."

"Good."

"What if I need to get in touch with you?"

"You should have no need to contact me before the exchange, so I will see you then."

"Well, how do I know that Vivian is okay?"

"Check your phone Mr. Hillis, and I will see you soon. Good-bye."

When Carwyn hung up, he had a video message waiting. It was Vivian, now dressed, holding the *New York Times* with the current date on it. She spoke briefly: "I am okay. I have been cut twice, but I have not been harmed or touched at all since then." When the video message ended, Carwyn hit the end button on his phone. *She is okay. At least she is okay.* But then he started to worry.

How the fuck was he going to get that kind of money? He had no savings of any kind. He certainly did not want to ask his mom to help. She couldn't contribute much anyway. He didn't have any other family or friends with liquid funds of that magnitude. Rebecca was the only person he knew who could possibly provide him with the amount of money he would need to save Vivian's life. *Rebecca.* Carwyn hadn't spoken to her since two or three weeks after Bret's funeral. He had never told her or Bret about Vivian. He did not look forward to going to her with an absurd request for over a million dollars. *It's my only option*, he thought. There was no other way.

He thought about doing nothing. Vivian had been out of his life for many months now, and she had even dated someone else. But doing nothing was not an option. Maybe he could rescue Vivian—fly over to Germany, overcome her captors, and bring her back to boring Montpelier where she would be safe. Was he sincerely considering such a crazy alternative? Yes, he was. He was considering and would continue to consider every option. Today was Friday. He had until Tuesday to come up with eight hundred thousand euros or to come up with some sort of plan to go in, guns blazing, and rescue Vivian from an unknown number of sick and twisted psychos. *Guns blazing?* He had never even fired a handgun. Was he serious? Yes. Yes, he was.

Would he have considered the same choice for a member of his family? Would he have done it for Bret? He wasn't sure that he would, and he was even less sure how that made him feel. Heartless? Weak? Unempathetic? Inhuman? Cruel? Scared? Soulless? Selfish? Well, none of that really mattered. He had to concentrate on the absurd task at hand. Carwyn knew, right then and there, that he would do everything in his power to make Vivian safe. The only question was whether everything in his power would be enough.

42

THE NEXT MORNING, AS Carwyn's wine headache faded (he had been unable to sleep before drinking a full bottle), he was able to focus on the insane, absolutely absurd, dreadful situation that he was now a part of. An incoming text message with the address for the exchange reinforced the reality of the situation.

During the night, Carwyn had dreamed of the Italian woman from the purgatory museum in Rome. In the dream, the woman repeated the words that she had first spoken to him in the museum. Even after waking, Carwyn remembered what she had said, almost as if Italian was his native tongue: *Se l'hai visto, significa che il tuo cuore si trova in purgatorio. Solo l'amore vero può salvare la tua anima.*

Carwyn had to guess at the spelling but was able to look up the phrase on a free language translation website. Essentially—if Carwyn had guessed right—the woman had advised him that if he had seen it, his heart was in purgatory and only true love could save him. Carwyn assumed that "it" referred to the twin-like apparition he had seen. *What better reason to go through hell?* he thought.

As he tried desperately to come up with some sort of plan, two things kept coming back to the forefront of his thoughts: first that he was not allowed to tell anyone, and second that there was a very good chance Mr. Not Important would kill Vivian even if Carwyn brought him all the money he had demanded.

While Carwyn didn't think Mr. Not Important would have a way of finding out if he actually told anyone, he was worried that they would kill Vivian. It was this fear more than any other sentiment (including the fear of putting his own life at risk) that helped Carwyn make up his mind. He would travel to Germany and save Vivian, or he would die trying.

Before the e-mail from Vivian, he had been hoping and wishing for something that might stem the anesthetic that seemed to have been dripping into his heart, mind, and soul. Well, he had that now: a cold shot of epinephrine to the core of his being. *Be careful what you wish for*, he thought. He wondered whether he would have made the decision to embark on a dangerous cross-continental rescue operation if frustration and anger had not been building inside him for the past couple months or more. As his thoughts wandered, Carwyn reflected on the woman from the purgatory museum and pondered whether she had foreseen any of this. He quickly dismissed the thought as somewhat nonsensical.

Carwyn decided that he would leave for Germany on Sunday. He had some serious preparation to do, but by leaving Sunday, he would have a full day in Nürnberg to do some reconnaissance and to psych himself up (and hopefully not psych himself out) for his brave, cosmically stupid, life-threatening, and life-affirming undertaking. *Where to begin?* Carwyn sat down and took several minutes to make a list.

First things first: Carwyn went online to purchase a one-way plane ticket. He was able to get a ticket for less than seven hundred bucks. He put it on his credit card. He would depart at around nine in the morning, but because of a two-hour layover at LaGuardia and another layover in Philadelphia, he wouldn't arrive in Nürnberg until a little after six in the morning local time on Monday. He would have plenty of time (he hoped) to assess the lay of the land. *What in the holy Kafkaesque fuck am I thinking?* He actually had that thought: *"holy Kafkaesque fuck."*

After he had purchased his plane ticket, Carwyn made a trip to his bank. His checking account balance was just a little over four thousand dollars. He went inside and up to the first available teller. Carwyn asked for the amount in all hundred-dollar bills. Four thousand dollars sure didn't look like all that much when presented in the form of forty hundred-dollar bills. His next stop was Wal-Mart. He bought the cheapest briefcase he could find and some sleeping pills for the plane. He figured he'd need to sleep on the plane in order to be awake and hopefully alert on the ground.

Once back home, Carwyn jumped back on the computer to rent a car and book a hotel room close to the address he had been provided. He had to pay extra for the rental car because he had never learned how to drive a manual transmission. The hotel room he booked was fairly cheap. *Probably a shit hole.* Once his car and room were reserved, he searched the internet for somewhere to purchase a bulletproof vest. He found nothing local. *Shit!* He gave more than passing consideration to the idea of going to the police station and stealing a vest. Maybe he could just ask to borrow one. *Yeah, right. Shit. Shit, shit, shit!*

While he was trying to figure out what to do about the vest, he dug out his small carry-on suitcase. He packed one pair of jeans, two shirts, two pairs each of socks and boxer briefs, and his black jacket with about a dozen pockets. He also tossed his cell phone charger into the suitcase. He decided he would wear his waterproof trail-running shoes, because they seemed like tough shoes. He would just wear them on the plane and save some space in his small suitcase. He put the shoes with the underwear, socks, jeans, and shirt that he planned to wear on the plane. Then he took his cell phone charger back out of his suitcase, plugged in his phone, and sat it on top of the clothes.

Now all he had to do was find a way to get his hands on a damn vest and figure out how he might get his hands on a gun or knife or both once in Germany. And he would have to exchange his dollars for euros at the airport. *A lot of planning goes into a rescue mission,* he thought with a laugh, but it was without any doubt a nervous laugh, because he almost threw up.

After searching the internet for about thirty-five minutes, Carwyn gave up on the idea of getting his hands on a gun (and hoped he hadn't been flagged on some sort of terrorist watch list). He determined, however, that he could get his hands on a knife in Germany. It looked like the bulletproof vest idea might have to go by the wayside too; he didn't have the time to wait for an online order to arrive. That made him nervous. He really liked the idea of a little extra protection.

Carwyn thought of a few more things he had not originally put on his list: binoculars, gloves, some form of pepper spray, and ingredients to make those firebomb things he had seen in several movies—the ones where a rag is stuffed into a bottle filled with gas or some other combustible liquid. He was really getting into this now.

Carwyn figured he wouldn't be able to take real pepper spray or bottle grenades on a plane, but he did have an idea for the pepper spray. He attempted to do an internet search of whether you could transfer pepper spray into an eyedrop container and whether that would be effective but didn't come up with anything.

What he did come across during his search were several recipes for homemade pepper spray. He combined the ingredients of three different recipes and started a new shopping list: habanero peppers, lemon juice, rubbing alcohol, bleach, baby oil. He added binoculars, gloves, and two spray bottles to the list.

He decided to look up the process of making the bottle grenades so that he would know what ingredients to acquire once he was in Germany. His search took about ten minutes before he finally came across anything actually useful. *Molotov cocktail—that's what it's called.* He was really going to be on a watch list now.

All he needed for the cocktails was empty glass bottles, cloth wicks, and gasoline. Further research introduced him to the idea of napalm and frag cocktails. He could use powdered sugar and ball bearings to make the cocktails more destructive. He wondered if adding something caustic might make them even nastier, so he added to his list glass bottles, cloth, gas, powdered sugar, ball bearings, acid. He put a question mark beside acid.

Back at home after his Bruce Willis shopping spree, Carwyn immediately set to the task of concocting his pepper spray. Carwyn's mom had gone to Montreal with her newish boyfriend Pierre, which was gross, but at least it meant she was out of the house for the weekend and Carwyn could avoid an interrogation. *Thank God.*

Carwyn put all the pepper spray ingredients except the bleach in a food processor and processed them as much as they would process. He then strained the mixture into a glass. To test the mixture, he poured just a little into one of his two spray bottles (one had originally held hair spray and the other lens cleaner—in hopes of avoiding any suspicion from TSA), spritzed a small amount into the air, and wafted it into his own face. "Yeah, shit, that will do the trick," he said to nobody.

Then Carwyn emptied the glass back into the processor, added the bleach, processed it some more, and strained the liquid back into the glass. Then he filled both of his spray bottles with the nasty concoction. Carwyn was impressed with himself.

Finally, he put the two seemingly innocent toiletries into a small Ziploc baggy, took the baggy to his room, and placed it with his clothes for tomorrow. Now everything had been marked off his list except the ingredients for his Molotov cocktails. He folded up the list and stuck it in his wallet. He had often wished that he was a spy when he was younger, and hell, even somewhat recently too. This was as close as he was ever going to get. *Too close.*

That night Carwyn couldn't sleep at all. He tossed and turned, his mind teeming with thoughts and misgivings. Adrenaline coursed through his veins like a class VI rapid. However, he stayed away from the wine this time. "What the hell am I doing?" he asked himself for the dozenth time. Tomorrow he would be embarking on one of the stupidest and most real trips he would probably ever take in his life. He should have sought out help beyond what Google had to offer. Despite his fear and agitation and overactive imagination, Carwyn finally drifted off to sleep sometime after 3:00 a.m.

Part 5

(NOW)

— 43 —

CARWYN'S CELL PHONE ALARM woke him at six in the morning, a mere three hours later than he had gotten to sleep. He showered quickly, got ready in eerie, surreal silence, and walked out the door at 6:24 a.m. It was generally about a forty-five minute drive up to the airport. Carwyn had one stop that he needed to make, and he wanted to get to the airport in plenty of time.

It turned out that even with his stop he had time to spare. Carwyn quickly discovered that sitting around in a less-than-bustling airport with nothing to do but wait to board a plane that may very well be flying you to the end of your days is not the most pleasant of ways to pass time.

Mercifully, an attendant finally called for boarding. Carwyn got in line as soon as his zone was called. It was about an hour-and-a-half flight to New York and then about an hour to Philadelphia. The layover time was fucking miserable. Carwyn bought food in both airports in an effort to use eating as an activity to pass the time. It didn't help all that much.

When Carwyn finally boarded the plane to Nürnberg, he was on the verge of going absolutely stir-bat-fucking-shit-crazy. He couldn't wait to pop his sleeping pills.

The in-flight meal was to be served about an hour into the flight. When the flight attendant came to get Carwyn's selection, Carwyn also asked for an (extremely overpriced) glass of red wine. While eating his meal, Carwyn took out his pills and read the bottle. The bottle said to take two, so Carwyn decided that taking four and washing them down with his red wine ought to do the trick.

Carwyn was not wrong. By the time he finished his meal, he was feeling a little loopy. Not long after he gave his trash to the flight attendant and put his tray table up, he was out like a light.

The next thing Carwyn was aware of was one of the overly perfumed flight attendants tapping him somewhat forcefully on the shoulder and repeating, "Sir, sir." Apparently it had taken more than just a couple light taps to wake him. Once up and off of the plane with his carry-on and empty briefcase, Carwyn became distinctly aware that he did not feel well at all. To the contrary, he felt like shit—really more like Jell-O. He felt like shit Jell-O. But he had a purpose.

Before doing anything else, Carwyn used his credit card to purchase a Coke. After gulping down his serving of caffeine, Carwyn located the currency exchange. He withdrew his forty crisp hundred-dollar bills. He was going to ask the attendant to give him all ones and twenties, but the smallest denomination was a five-euro note. That really screwed up his plan.

His plan had been to make stacks of one-euro notes with twenty-euro notes on top as decoys. That certainly wasn't going to happen. Making matters worse, his $4,000 would yield only a little over 3,000 euros. Making matters worse still, no two euro denominations were the same size. It was right then and there that Carwyn realized the decoy portion of his plan was simply not going to work. *Fuck.*

He should have done a bit more research. Hell, he shouldn't have even needed to do research; it wasn't like he had never been to Europe before. His nerves were barely holding up. He would have to come up with another idea. The guy at the exchange window was looking at him quizzically. Carwyn realized that he had been standing there for too long without saying or doing anything.

"May I help you, sir?" said the attendant, correctly inferring from the hundred-dollar bills in Carwyn's hand that he spoke English.

"Um, yes. I want to get some euros, please," said Carwyn and handed the man his bills.

The man counted Carwyn's bills and punched a couple of buttons on a computer.

"You will get 2,973 euros."

"What?"

"With the current exchange rate and the transaction fee, your dollars will yield 2,973 Euros."

"Fine." Carwyn was not happy, but he really didn't have any other option. All the exchange centers would likely have the same fees. Thinking on his feet about what denominations he might be able to use to have some type of decoy effect, Carwyn said, "Can I get four five hundreds, two hundreds, six fifties, um, six twenties, seventy fives, and three one-euro coins?"

The attendant punched a couple more buttons on his computer, put Carwyn's U.S. dollars in a drawer, and then withdrew some euros and began to count them out. He counted out the appropriate amount of euro notes and then plucked the one-euro coins from a coin dispenser and handed the money to Carwyn with a small receipt.

Carwyn took the money, walked over to the nearest bench, and sat down. He opened his empty briefcase, quickly stuffed his new euros into one of the small back pockets, and then closed the briefcase. Even though his briefcase contained far less than eight hundred thousand euros, Carwyn was still nervous to be caring that much money in the middle of a foreign country. Carrying less than three thousand euros around in a briefcase at the airport would be the least of Carwyn's worries over the next couple of days.

After his first dose of caffeine and after exchanging his money, Carwyn decided to get a second dose of caffeine in the form of a coffee. He was able to attach his briefcase to his carry-on so that he could walk and sip his coffee at the same time. Coffee in hand, he proceeded directly to the car rental pick-up. Thankfully, there was an available attendant, and Carwyn did not have to wait in line. Carwyn completed his transaction and had keys in hand in about ten minutes. He was surprised that his car was actually an American car—probably because he had to splurge on an automatic transmission.

Once in his rental car, Carwyn retrieved his preprinted hotel confirmation and directions. He had never driven a car in a foreign country, but at least he was able to drive on the right side of the road. He drove directly to his hotel and checked in. It was a bit of a shit hole. The clock in his room informed him that it was only 8:09 a.m. Knife time.

Carwyn drove approximately twenty minutes to the place he had previously found online. He was not disappointed. Carwyn browsed for about fifteen minutes or so and decided to purchase two folding knives, one fairly small and one bigger with a partially serrated blade. It cost ninety euros, which meant he was more than one hundred dollars closer to maxing out his credit card.

The next destination was the exchange site. Carwyn had previously mapped out a route to the address. From the knife store, it took him about half an hour to get to the predetermined address. He had been so busy getting his shit together that it wasn't until he drove past the exchange site that he experienced fear for the first time since arriving in Nürnberg.

Carwyn drove past the seemingly abandoned building one more time somewhat slowly but not *too* slowly. After checking out the exchange site and getting lost on his way back to his hotel, Carwyn did not get back up to his room until after twelve. He was hungry. He didn't want to waste time procuring food but knew he should eat. He drove around until he found a McDonald's. Maybe he just needed the comfort of those golden arches. When he was done eating, it was time to go cocktail shopping.

He drove around until he found a large grocery store. He had his list at the ready. Into his cart went a six-pack of beer. That would serve the dual purpose of calming his nerves and providing the containers for his firebombs. Next he hunted around for powdered sugar. It was easier to find than he might have thought. He didn't think he would find ball bearings, so he looked for a hardware section in the grocery store. He was somewhat surprised to find one, but he happily added a package of small nails to his cart.

Next on his list was acid. *Drain Cleaner!* It was like an epiphany. Carwyn hurried to a home products aisle and had to use the pictures to ascertain which jug was drain cleaner. Once he had it figured out, he added it to his cart. The ominous warning symbols pleased him. After he located a lighter, he was ready to check out.

Carwyn stopped at a gas station on his way back to his hotel. He purchased a gas can and filled it with gasoline. It was almost four in the afternoon. *Already? Shit.* Time was flying. Surely that was better than just waiting, waiting, waiting.

Up in his hotel room, Carwyn set to work preparing. First he opened a beer and chugged it. Then he opened another one to drink at a more reasonable pace. He laid out his socks, shoes, underwear, jeans, shirt, jacket, and gloves on the small table in his room. He opened up his two knives, practiced flipping them open and folding them closed a few times, and then placed them on the table.

Next he put his two pepper spray bottles and his lighter on the table beside the knives. He finished his second beer. He rinsed out the two empty beer bottles (making sure to keep the caps) and set them upside-down on the bathroom sink to dry. He sat the gasoline can, the drain cleaner, the powdered sugar, and the package of nails on the sink near the bottles. He took the cloth that he was going to use for wicks back into the main room and used one of his new knives to cut six strips. He placed the strips next to everything else on the bathroom sink.

It was about 5:00 p.m. Carwyn opened his third beer and turned on the TV. Since all the TV shows were in German, Carwyn flipped the channels until he came across a music video channel. The distraction was warmly welcomed. After finishing his third beer, Carwyn took it to the bathroom, rinsed it out, and set it upside-down.

Then he set the other two bottles upright, poured enough sugar in each to cover the bottom, added the drain cleaner, sloshed it around to mix with the sugar, dropped about one-sixth of the nails into each, and filled each up to the tapered neck with gasoline. Two Molotov cocktails were basically ready to go. *Now what?* With just under twenty-seven hours until tomorrow's scheduled exchange was supposed to take place, Carwyn would have a lot of uneasy waiting to do.

It started getting dark sometime after six o'clock. Carwyn was getting restless, a product of nerves more than anything. *Well, dinner time it is.* Carwyn decided to walk. It would help pass more time. After ambling, without any destination in mind for twenty minutes, he found a decent-enough-looking place and ventured inside. His waitress was quite pleasant and spoke English. She helped him select a good dark beer and a traditional dish for his dinner. He drank two beers with his dinner.

He sat lost in indeterminate thought for some time. His waitress, as was the European custom, was perfectly content to let him sit unattended to. After a while, she did come by and ask if he wanted anything else. Carwyn just asked for his check. He paid, and as he stood to leave, he couldn't help wondering, *What if Bret and I had gone to Munich before going to Amsterdam?* Asking what if is a dangerous, often unwinnable game.

Night had fully descended upon the city while Carwyn was dining. The air had cooled, and Carwyn was anxious to get back to his hotel room and his sleeping pills. About half a block from his hotel, Carwyn's text message alert startled him and literally made him jump. He was definitely on edge. Carwyn opened the message as he continued to walk to his hotel. The message read, "Change of plans" and provided a different exchange address. It also set a new time for 11:00 p.m., three hours later than the previous time. *Do they know I'm here? Do they know I scouted out the building?*

Carwyn's fear kicked into overdrive, but there was something inside him, some unconscious psychological and biophysiological mechanism, working hard to maintain a sense of calm and sanity. Carwyn continued on to his hotel, where he asked the man at the desk if there was an internet café nearby. The man spoke very little English, and it was a struggle to communicate with him, but Carwyn was finally able to determine that there was a twenty-four-hour internet place three blocks from his hotel. He went straight there.

Carwyn paid for half an hour, the smallest increment that could be selected, and sat down at an antiquated machine. It served his purpose though. Carwyn mapped the route from his hotel to the new address he had been provided; it was about an hour away. The distance did not help his nerves. Still, he knew that he must not falter in his resolve. He printed out the map and directions, paid way too much for the pages, and walked back to his hotel. Up in his room, he made sure to hang the Do Not Disturb sign on the door.

Carwyn's nerves were well frazzled. It was as if a horde of nanoscopic rats was attempting to chew its way out of the maze of Carwyn's mind. He didn't want to think about the task at hand anymore that evening. He opened all three of his remaining beers. He downed one quickly, and then he washed down two sleeping pills (four had been a bit much) with another beer.

Carwyn forgot to take into account the multiple beers he had imbibed that evening, and somewhere between the fifth and sixth beer from his six-pack, he passed out. Tomorrow would be a very long day, but it could be a very short night.

— 44 —

CARWYN WALKED—MORE LIKE MARCHED—TO his rental car. He didn't even know what time it was. And then, without even being aware of unlocking the car, settling into the driver's seat, or starting the engine, he was on the road.

He had received new directions and was headed, as he discovered after a twenty-minute drive, to an old, abandoned warehouse in a forgotten part of the city. He arrived about fifteen minutes early, but there were already three large men waiting for him beside a dark gray Mercedes station wagon. Carwyn put his car in park but did not shut off the engine.

One of the men brought his hand up to his throat and made a back and forth slashing motion. Carwyn assumed the gesture meant that he was to turn off his car, but he thought about playing dumb. However, since all three men had guns and Carwyn did not know where Vivian was being kept, he decided to comply. Once the rental car's engine was off, the silence seemed to creep into Carwyn's bones. The silence was downright scary.

Now that it was silent, one of the men yelled at Carwyn to get out of the car with his hands in the air. The man had a thick accent. *Why did I ever think that this was a good idea?* Carwyn got out of his shitty little rental car with his arms and hands raised to the heavens, almost as if he was reaching out for some divine intervention. God wasn't watching on this night. No help was going to come from on high.

One of the men had a pistol trained on Carwyn. The other two walked quickly over to Carwyn's car. One retrieved the two briefcases. The other leaned into the driver's side, plucked the keys from the ignition, and placed them in his pocket. The man who had taken the briefcases out of the car walked around to Carwyn and, without saying a word, handed them both to him. *Smart.* If Carwyn was carrying the briefcases, he couldn't really do anything else with his hands, couldn't do anything stupid.

"Walk," said one of the men. Carwyn started walking with one of the men on his left side and the other on his right. The man with the gun led the way into the warehouse. Carwyn felt like a death-row inmate making the long walk, the final walk, to the execution chamber. Carwyn couldn't even remember what he had eaten for dinner just a few short hours before, so it must not have been all that great of a last meal.

The man with the gun stopped in front of a small table and then walked around to the other side. "Place the money on the table," he commanded.

Carwyn was overtly nervous. He had no idea how he would possibly get out of this mess. He placed the briefcases on the table and then stuck his hands in his pockets so he could feel the knives he had purchased earlier.

"Hands out of pockets. Now!" ordered one of the men in a gruff eastern European accent.

Carwyn noticed for the first time an office on the second floor of the warehouse. There were no windows; they had probably long ago been broken. There was at least one other man in the office, and Carwyn could barely make out the figure of someone seated in a chair with a bag of some sort covering her head. *That must be Vivian.*

"Open the cases," said the man with the gun.

Carwyn didn't know what to do. If he opened the cases, that would mean certain death. He considered his alternatives. *Fight?* There were the Molotov cocktails, and he had his lighter in his pocket. And he had his knives. *Well, here goes nothing,* he thought.

"What are you waiting for?"

"Nothing. Sorry."

But the brief delay had elicited more than impatience. It had aroused suspicion.

Carwyn could almost feel the laser sight on him as the mood in the room changed, became almost palpably violent. He looked down, and sure enough, there was a red dot glowing on his chest right about where his heart was hammering. He couldn't see the dot wavering on his forehead, where his brain was trying to process, to think, to plan, to arrive at some miraculous idea for saving his and Vivian's lives.

Just before he reached into his pockets for his knives, Carwyn thought of something that might buy him just a whisper of an opportunity.

"They both require a key. The keys are in my pockets."

"Get the fucking keys—slowly—then open the fucking cases."

Slowly. Perfect. He could flip open his knives and have them at the ready. He took a half-step back with his right foot and tried to look like he was fishing for his keys. When he had the knives open, Carwyn pulled them from his pockets and thrust his arms back all in one fluid motion. The knives lodged into the thighs of both men, who gasped in pain. Carwyn snatched the case that held the Molotov cocktails from the table as he kicked the table into the man with the gun. Shots started to ring out, but the table provided some distraction—and some cover.

Carwyn darted into a dark corner behind some old, broken-down piece of machinery. He felt like he was in a time warp. He opened his case and lit one of the cloth cocktail wicks as bullets thunked into the metal all around him. He chucked the cocktail at the table and ducked out of the way. It exploded, but Carwyn caught a bullet in the forearm. It was a through and through shot.

Behind his makeshift barricade, Carwyn lit another cocktail and reared back to launch it toward the man in the windowless office about forty feet away. But then he hesitated. *Vivian was up there.* And again he could sense the laser sight. In the instant before the gunman pulled the trigger, Carwyn looked to see the red dot of death dancing over his heart. Then the music stopped. The dot was still. Carwyn heard the bang, bang, bang of several shots being fired.

The bullets tore through his flesh, ripped through his muscle, and splintered some bone. One of the bullets went clean through. A couple lodged in his gut. But for at least one of the shots (probably the very first one), the laser sight was true, and one of the bullets pierced his hammering heart.

As Carwyn fell forward almost as if in slow motion, another couple of rounds were fired. One of the bullets took off half of his left cheek, and the other rifled through his neck. Carwyn would never know what sorts of despicable things the surviving men (hopefully between the knife wounds and the Molotov cocktail Carwyn had killed at least one of the bastards) would do to Vivian. He was dead before he hit the cold, hard, dirty, blood-sodden floor. The last thing he saw was his ghostly, darker-haired twin—the one from the purgatory museum—reaching out to him from below.

— 45 —

As it turned out, even though Carwyn had technically been cleared, officer Rossi, who had always had a tendency to get paranoid, had been intermittently monitoring Carwyn and his activities. One of the tracking devices Aeneid had planted had been in Carwyn's luggage, specifically the bag Carwyn used as his carry-on bag for his flight to Germany. Even TSA hadn't detected it.

When officer Rossi noticed that Carwyn was in New York and then in Philadelphia, he told Lorenz. Seizing the opportunity to get rid of another possible threat, Lorenz informed Johnny, and Johnny got nervous. When it was clear that Carwyn was on his way to Europe, Aeneid was dispatched on the next flight to Paris to await further instructions.

Paris was a somewhat central location, and once it was clear where Carwyn was headed, Aeneid could get to his location quickly. From Paris it was not much longer than a two-hour flight to most major cities in Western Europe.

Aeneid had not yet been given an order to eliminate Carwyn; however, she suspected that it would not be long before such an order was given. If need be, she was ready for whatever she had to do.

— 46 —

CARWYN JOLTED AWAKE, SWEATING profusely, his heart racing, his head pounding. He stank of beer. *It was only a dream—a nightmare.* Carwyn had never actually died in a dream before. He had always woken before the decisive moment. He was shaken and a little bit freaked out, but he was alive.

There were two empty beer bottles on the nightstand and one on the floor. He must have passed out and spilled beer on himself. He had an absolute bitch of a headache. It was like his head was in a fog, the fog had a heart beat, the beating heart was a runaway freight train, and the train's manifest consisted solely of wild elephants, none of which had been sedated—and all of which were feverishly attempting to break free of the confines of the train and escape the fog. The pounding and the pressure in his skull were beyond severe and consuming. He was literally incapable of any high level thinking.

When Carwyn moved to get out of the bed, the train slammed into the back of his head and some of the elephants got loose. He plodded to the bathroom and, as gross as the tub looked, ran a hot bath. As soon as the tub was full enough, Carwyn stripped out of his clothes, each movement ratcheting up the intensity of the pain in his head, and plopped himself down into the almost-too-hot water. Carwyn turned the knobs to cut off the water flow about thirty seconds later and let himself sink up to his nose in the tub.

The hot water slowly acted as a sedative for the pissed-off elephants, gently applied the brakes to the freight train, and even burned off the fog to some degree. Carwyn's head felt better. But it sure as hell didn't feel good. As he remained soaking in the hot, healing water, Carwyn couldn't help but wonder how he and Vivian had become Mr. Not Important's targets. Was it because of somebody at his hostel in Amsterdam? Somebody from his blackout experience in Moscow? The

Russian cabbie? Somebody altogether different and random? Carwyn realized he would probably never know for sure.

Carwyn started to doze and sink down under the warm water, but he was jolted awake by a muffled voice whispering, "Se l'hai visto, significa che il tuo cuore si trova in purgatorio. Solo l'amore vero può salvare la tua anima." He realized he must have hallucinated the voice, but he couldn't quite shake a lingering preternatural feeling.

When Carwyn could feel his fingers and toes starting to get pruney, he decided it was time to get out of the tub. He didn't check the time until after he was dried and dressed. It was after 2:00 p.m. *Holy shit*, he thought, although the time was perfectly okay with him: the less time to sit and think and worry the better.

He put the three empty beer bottles upside-down to dry and went on a mission for the crispy, golden, healing goodness of McDonald's french fries. His American fast-food lunch, coupled with some German pain killers, more or less completed his healing process. Now he was about as ready as he could possibly be for the rest of the day.

Carwyn went back up to his room to get the printout of the directions to the new drop spot—and his knives, just in case. He decided not to take his pepper spray or any of the firebombs on his reconnaissance mission.

Following the directions took him first to the edge of and then into the middle of what he thought must be the Black Forest. He hadn't seen any signs to either confirm or contradict his belief, and once surrounded by trees, it could have been the damn Sherwood Forest for all he knew. *Where is Robin Hood when you need him?*

Carwyn figured that the change of location had been part of the plan the whole time. Driving to the new address brought him to a hotel. *Surely they aren't going to conduct the exchange here. What a waste of time.* Carwyn figured he had further instructions coming and drove straight back to his hotel.

After mixing up the last four Molotov cocktails and searching for the missing sixth cap—it was under the bed—Carwyn used the smaller of his two knives to cut a tiny hole in each of the six bottle caps. The clock in his room declared that the time was 6:03 p.m. He decided he should go ahead and get things ready. First he changed his clothes and put on his shoes. Then he put his knives, pepper spray, lighter, and gloves into his jacket.

Next he fashioned two decoy stacks of money with one five-hundred-euro note on each side and secured them in the briefcase. He wondered if he'd have been better off robbing a bank to actually get the money. *Shit, shit, shit, shit!*

Carwyn hadn't yet figured out how he was going to transport his firebombs. He hoped his fifth and sixth hamburgers in two days would give him an idea. The best idea he could come up with while dining in the familiar confines of a German McDonald's was to tape them inside his briefcase—and then make sure the briefcase remained upright at all times. After eating, he looked for a place to buy some duct tape.

When he got back to the hotel room, it was 7:28 p.m. Carwyn doused his cloth wicks in gas. Technically, using gas wasn't what his internet research had told him to do, but surely it would work just the same. When the wicks had all been soaked, he shoved them through the holes he had cut in the bottle caps, pushed them down into the bottles, and then put the caps on. Then he taped around the neck and cap of each bottle to keep the caps securely fastened. He was taping the bottles into the briefcase when a text message came in: "Same place, different time: 9:00. Further instructions to follow."

They were just fucking with him now. But his Molotov cocktails were ready, he hoped. He put the potentially very explosive case upright by the door. He put his jacket on, checked that his directions were in his pocket, and then went straight to the toilet and puked his guts out. Leaving the bathroom, he stopped to look at himself in the mirror. For a flickering instant, he didn't even recognize himself. *Can I really do this?*

He went back into the bedroom area. He set one of his pillows up in the lone chair in the room. He took a few steps back and then walked up to the pillow. He took out his knife, adroitly flipped it open, and stabbed the pillow with a cold, detached, forceful vengeance.

A pillow was certainly not a person, but he had never stabbed anyone or anything before, and he had to try to get rid of any hesitation now. He walked over to the pillow still on the bed and, ramping up the malice, not only stabbed it but gutted it of the shitty-quality, neck-cramp-inducing stuffing inside it. If he was walking into a pillow fight, he felt confident that he would be unstoppable. He just hoped he could act as decisively and as violently when there was skin and hair and fat and muscle and tendons and bones and blood involved, when both his and Vivian's life depended on his actions.

After psyching himself up on the pillows, Carwyn grabbed his briefcase and walked out the hotel room door. The night was already dark and cool. Carwyn had been afraid of the dark as a kid. The dark of this night was scarier than any darkness from his youth or from any other time in his life. It was as if the night had thousands of sinister eyes, and they were all watching him.

— 47 —

THROUGH THE WINDOWS OF Carwyn's crappy little rental car, the generic but sinister landscape passed by, vanishing into oblivion in one ominous green and gray and black blur. Carwyn wondered whether it was the end of his life or the true beginning that he was approaching as fast as the landscape was passing by.

Carwyn arrived at the initial destination at around 8:45 p.m. He parked in between two other cars in a dimly lit section of the parking lot and waited for either a text message or a bullet to the brain. Carwyn reacted as if he had been shot when his phone vibrated at 9:01 p.m. His further instructions were: "Leave the hotel parking lot. Turn right. Drive 15 km. Turn left. Drive 9 km. Turn right onto dirt road. Drive 6 km. Turn right. Drive 2 km. Stop. Wait."

That was another thirty-two kilometers—about twenty miles, give or take. On these roads at night, not really knowing where he was going, that might take another forty-five minutes or even an hour. And stopping and waiting in the middle of the woods for a posse of psychos was certainly not his idea of a good time. Before leaving the hotel, he made the judgment call to take three of his Molotov cocktails out of his briefcase and wedge them upright between the passenger seat and the center console.

And then, as a result of his nerves and multiple hamburgers, in one of the most surreal experiences of his life, Carwyn had to walk nonchalantly through the very fancy hotel lobby and find a men's bathroom in order to deal with a case of the nervous shits.

At 9:56 Carwyn made his final turn onto an even smaller dirt road than the one on which he had been driving. He came to a stop at 9:58 p.m. but didn't turn off the car. Then he waited. There was nothing else to do. Every slight sound that he heard made him jump. All of his senses were working in overdrive: he was seeing and hearing things that weren't actually there, and he could see, smell, hear, feel, and even taste violence in the air.

Once, he caught a glance of his own reflection in the rental car's driver side window and reached for one of his knives, but he quickly realized it was his own reflected image. Under different circumstances, he would have probably laughed out loud at himself, but instead he concentrated on trying to get his heart to stop beating so fast.

Minutes and lifetimes later, at 10:30 p.m., the headlights of what could have been any piece-of-junk car approached from the distance and then morphed, as the car got closer, into the headlights of a very expensive-looking automobile with darkly tinted windows. The car stopped multiple car lengths away from Carwyn and turned on its high beams, making it very difficult for Carwyn to see anything at all in front of him.

Carwyn knew right then and there that this cold and deathly quiet night was going to erupt into no-turning-back violence, that the seemingly sanguine shell of serenity was going to shatter into a thousand knife-sharp shards, shredding the very atmosphere of the night. The sanguine was certain to become sanguinary. Blood. Would. Flow.

But he did not feel fear. Perhaps he had worried and puked and even shat it all out. Now he simply maintained a quiet resolve.

He could have taken one of his cocktails and hurled it at the expensive car right then, but he didn't know if Vivian was inside. If she was a passenger, she would likely be hurt or even killed. Even if she wasn't in the car, if Carwyn firebombed it, he might never find her. Again he found his only option was to wait.

Carwyn didn't have to wait long: his phone chirped, and the new text message icon appeared on the screen. It read, "If you have the necessary funds to complete the transaction, flash your headlights once." Carwyn flashed his lights, and then he received another text message: "Get out of your car, place the money on the hood, and then walk toward the other vehicle."

Carwyn didn't know what to do. If someone from the other car checked the money now, he was screwed, probably dead. *Wait, the* other *vehicle—not* my *vehicle. Maybe the ringleader, Mr. Not Important, isn't in that car. That means Vivian is probably not in there either.*

Carwyn's mind raced. *What do I do? Firebomb the car?* It was likely that would create too much noise, and the fire might be seen from afar, alerting Vivian's other captors to a problem and costing Vivian her life. *Rush the car?* If Carwyn did that, it was likely one of the expensive car's ruthless passengers would shoot him down. *Fuck*, he thought, and then he repeated out loud, "Fuck, fuck, fuck."

Carwyn was suddenly cognizant of the fact that he had already taken too long to get out of the car as the last text message had directed. He opened his door, grabbed the briefcase, placed it on the hood of his shitty rental car, and started walking toward the unknown of the car idling in front of him. After Carwyn had taken only a couple of steps, the other car's passenger door opened, and a very large man got out. "Get in the passenger seat," he said as he walked right past Carwyn on his way to Carwyn's rental car and the less than three thousand euros and three Molotov cocktails in the briefcase.

Carwyn thought about launching himself at the large man as they passed each other, but then the driver of the car would probably simply get out and shoot him. *And there might be other men in the car.* Carwyn knew he couldn't just go getting himself killed now. The one thing that he had going for him, his one advantage, was the element of surprise.

Carwyn got into the car. The only other man inside was the driver. He had to act quickly. He pulled both knives, which he had already flipped open, from his pocket, lunged at the driver, and stabbed him in both the neck and the leg, hopping to get lucky and hit either the carotid or the femoral artery. He was *very* lucky; his desperate lunging and stabbing and slicing opened up both major arteries. There was a lot of blood—much more than Carwyn had ever seen in person. If he hadn't been running on adrenaline and desperation, he might have thrown up again.

It took Carwyn too long to push the driver's dead weight out of the car to the cold, hard ground. He was going to put the car in drive and run over the other man, but the large man had heard, or maybe just sensed, the commotion of Carwyn's desperate attack—and he had also opened Carwyn's briefcase. The man was removing his cell phone from his pocket when he turned and saw Carwyn in the driver seat. He deftly pulled a silencer-equipped pistol from a shoulder holster that was concealed under his jacket. Before Carwyn could hit the gas, the large man, holding his cell phone in one hand and his gun in the other, fired several rounds, shattering the expensive car's windshield and hitting Carwyn square in the chest.

— 48 —

AENEID HAD DONE A lot of thinking before boarding the plane to Paris and even more thinking during the flight. *Seriously? Fucking France?* The flight was a red-eye, but she simply couldn't sleep. A lot of shit had been fucked up lately. She had not been making good decisions. She felt that she had lost the integrity that differentiated her from dirty cops like Lorenz and other sundry pieces of shit. She didn't know exactly when or how or why things had gone all wrong. She couldn't account for when or how or why she had lost herself.

There was only one thing she could think of that might make things less wrong—not right, not right at all, but less wrong. She could never make things right.

Aeneid had only packed a small overnight bag. Before she embarked for Paris, she had cut and died her hair and retrieved an alias packet (passport, IDs, and other necessaries in an assumed name and nationality) from a safety deposit box. She had made one very important phone call, and then she had walked about ten blocks from her apartment and called a taxi from a payphone. Even though the *gentiluomini* knew her general itinerary, she'd become paranoid and hadn't wanted anybody to follow her. She might not be able to travel back in time, but she could push forward. And from here on out, she intended to do things her way.

49

ALTHOUGH HE WAS UPSET that he had been forced to kill the man that was now sitting in the driver seat (the boss had wanted him alive, even if he hadn't brought the money) and pissed that the briefcase did not contain eight hundred thousand euros, the large hulk of a man who had shot Carwyn walked coolly back to the car, typing a text to his boss as he walked. The hulk was also pissed that he would have to lug the cheap asshole out of the driver seat, likely getting blood on his suit.

*   *   *   *

Meanwhile, Carwyn could barely breathe, and his chest was on fire. But he was alive—so far—which was an infinitely better outcome than in his dream. It felt like he had at least one cracked or broken rib. Carwyn was thanking God and Buddha and Jesus and especially Rick, the pony-tailed, flannel-clad cashier at the gunsmith in Colbyville. The bulletproof vest Rick had sold Carwyn had just done its job.

Through pain-squinted eyes, Carwyn could see the hulk of a man approaching, cell phone in hand. Carwyn figured that he was probably calling or texting Mr. Not Important to inform him that Carwyn did not have the money. Carwyn could not let any such call or text go through. Carwyn cut his eyes upward and met the large psycho hulk's murderous gaze. In that instant they each knew what the other was going to do.

Carwyn shifted the car into drive, slouched down, and got as low as he could. He hit the gas as the hulk opened fire. One bullet grazed Carwyn's arm, but the hulk's aim was thrown off by the car speeding at him, and none of the other rounds hit the intended target. The man jumped out of the way, and Carwyn slammed into his own rental car. Luckily he hadn't had the time to get up to a very high rate of speed.

From off to the side of the car, the man fired several more shots. One round took off one of the expensive car's side mirrors. Carwyn was slightly dazed by the force of the impact but managed to roll out of the car as the man fired yet again. Carwyn wasn't sure, but he thought he heard a faint click. Maybe the fucker was out of bullets.

Seizing what was likely his only opportunity, Carwyn charged, knives out. The man kicked Carwyn square in the knee with the heel of his right boot. When Carwyn tumbled to the ground, the man kicked the knives out of his hands, breaking Carwyn's left pinky finger in the process. He couldn't feel any pain in either of his hands. His brain was too preoccupied with his knee.

He had felt and heard what seemed like every ligament and tendon in his knee tearing. The sound and sensation of it almost made him puke. The pain was somewhat delayed, but then, as if his knee was an explosive at the end of a lengthy fuse, it hit him. It was like the lovechild of napalm and some sharp medieval instrument of death, searing and stabbing through his entire leg.

Time seemed to be standing still, but in reality Carwyn knew it was passing in a torrent. "Son of a bitch," he muttered through gritted teeth. *How can I save Vivian now?* he desperately wondered. He knew there had to be others who were holding her captive at some location who knew how far away from where he was now. Her life (and his) teetered on a razor's edge. A boot to Carwyn's midsection produced a hollow thud and a barely audible crack. *There goes another rib or two.* Carwyn coughed, but only a little spittle dangled from his lip—no blood.

Carwyn still didn't know what the shit he'd been thinking. In a way, though, he had just fallen into this situation. Rather, he had been pushed. For the past several months—and really, even before that—everything in his life had been building up to this point. Carwyn scoured the ground around him for his knives or any other weapon. *This is it,* he thought. *I am actually going to die.*

And then came yet another kick to his ribs. This time a little blood formed at Carwyn's lips as a painful litany of coughs escaped his mouth from somewhere deep inside him. If he had been able to register emotions, he would have been officially scared shitless.

He thought if only he had enough power to turn his litany of coughing into a litany of swear words—or even just grunts—then he might also be able to summon the necessary strength and energy from somewhere in the cold universe to make one final attempt to save not only his own life but a life that he had at least briefly considered to be just as—if not more—important than his own. *Vivian!* The thought exploded into his consciousness and seemed to surge through his body as if Vivian's name and essence were in Carwyn's blood.

Another kick veered in toward Carwyn's midsection and his already aching, probably cracked—if not broken—ribs. Carwyn had seemingly misapprehended his level of completely ass-kicked-ness and bodily injury.

His movements were reflexive. His arms sprang like a mouse trap and wrapped around his would-be-murderer's leg. His mind reeled, worked in overdrive: *His leg is a mouse; does that make my stomach the cheese?* And Carwyn actually laughed. *What the fuck am I thinking? Do people really laugh when they are getting beaten to death? What do I do? How—shit, I have to do something now: jump, kick, bite, spin, stand. If I could stand, that would be a miracle. This is the only glimmer of light in the steadily closing darkness of death: do something, do something, act now, fuck …*

His mind completely shut off as his body began to act. He literally didn't have enough energy to think and act at the same time. *So act.* With his hulking attacker's leg in his arms, he quickly rolled over with as much force as his body could generate. The attacker lost his balance and fell hard to the ground. He landed squarely on his open cell phone, more or less crushing it under his weight, and he dropped his gun. Carwyn had hoped to break the man's leg, but he did not have enough power left in his body to break a thick, strong leg bone.

Carwyn rolled over on top of the man. He let his elbow fall with all his weight onto the man's face, and he was a little bit lucky. The man's nose broke under the weight of Carwyn's bony elbow, and blood squirted from it almost as if his nose was a ketchup packet that some bratty kid had squeezed too hard when he didn't get the toy he wanted in his happy meal. *I need to keep going.* Carwyn began to flail wildly.

He wasn't hitting the man hard enough for it to be described as pummeling. *Shit, this isn't working—what can I do? Eyes.* Carwyn allowed his full weight to fall on his hands, with his fingers aimed directly at the man's eyes. The man was able to block one, but he couldn't block both. Carwyn's right index finger plunged into the man's left eye.

Carwyn could actually feel the eye break or pop or squish— whatever you called it when an eye gets poked with all the force and waning strength one desperate human being can muster and that eye does something really gross that it is definitely not supposed to do. Carwyn would have surely puked then if he hadn't been hyped up on adrenaline, fear, desperation, anger, and a glimmer of hope. Whether as a result of some divine force or something much more mundane, Carwyn could feel more energy stretching through his bones and joints and veins. And the man was definitely dazed by his eye problem. Carwyn reinitiated his punching. Now you could call it pummeling—just barely. *I have to kill this guy,* he thought. He actually thought it, and it actually gave him pause.

He hadn't really thought about the first life he had taken about ten minutes—and one lifetime—ago. Part of him wanted to do it, to kill this man. Part of him was actually excited to do it and relished the thought. However, there was another part that didn't want to and that felt almost queasy at the thought. The somewhat primitive idea of literally beating another human being to death with his bare hands made Carwyn hesitate.

That instant of indecision was all it took for Mr. Not Important's large henchman to regain his violent momentum. Although he had a broken nose and a jellied, bloodied eye, the man sat up and head butted Carwyn square in the jaw. The blow knocked out one of Carwyn's teeth; worse than that, it knocked Carwyn unconscious.

The man dragged Carwyn to the back of the car. He popped the trunk and removed a role of duct tape. There was nothing else in the trunk for precisely this type of situation. He wouldn't want there to be anything in the trunk that any unwilling passenger could ever use as a weapon.

The man took his time taping Carwyn's hands together behind his back and taping his feet together. As a final measure, he placed a strip of duct tape across Carwyn's mouth. He made sure to leave his nose uncovered so Carwyn could breath. Although he had thought he had killed Carwyn moments earlier, the man didn't want him to die now—at least not yet. His boss would definitely want to make some use of him first.

After he was done with his tape job, the man lifted Carwyn and heaved him into the trunk. He slammed the trunk shut as a slimy, sly smile slithered across his face. Although English was not his native language, there was one phrase that had worked itself into the hulk's vocabulary: "Fuck you."

50

ABOUT FIVE OR SO minutes into the drive to where Vivian was being held, Carwyn regained consciousness and experienced a wide range of emotions: anger, fear, frustration, hatred, loneliness, longing, anxiety, nervousness, and—about ten minutes too late—murderous rage. Carwyn decided that he no longer had any qualms about killing the driver. *But how?*

The undercurrent of love (Carwyn couldn't help but wonder whether his dire situation had clarified his feelings or created them) and Carwyn's desire to protect Vivian helped to keep him thinking. If he had been totally overpowered by his newly cemented wish to kill the motherfucker in the driver's seat, he might not have been able to think at all—not that too many good ideas were flowing through his mind anyway.

Carwyn painfully writhed and stretched in a blind attempt to search the trunk for anything he could use as a weapon. *Nothing. Fuck.* His thoughts were so frantic that Carwyn wondered if he had actually yelled them out loud. Carwyn knew, however, that he could only rely on one thing: the element of surprise. The one glimmer of hope he clung to was that the psycho bastard would assume he was still unconscious.

Suddenly, Carwyn became aware of a deafening silence. The car had stopped, and the engine was cut off. They were there—wherever there was. Where Vivian was.

Up to this very moment Carwyn had pushed almost everybody he'd ever cared about away. Surely he wouldn't do that to someone he was willing to get shot at, kicked in the ribs, and shoved in a trunk for. He wished he could know now whether he would end up pushing Vivian away at some point down the road. Scratch that: knowing how things would end at some future point in time would

have drained all the purpose and desire out of
life.

There had been times in the past when Carwyn had wished he could foresee the future. The pragmatist in him knew, however, that even if one could see into the future, surely one wouldn't be able to foresee only personally selected moments in time. The full expanse of that which was yet to be, but which would be—the good and the bad—would be visible to the mind's eye. Presently Carwyn had absolutely no wish to see into the future. He desired simply to shape it—starting now.

$$* \quad * \quad * \quad *$$

Out of desperation and an absence of alternatives, Carwyn settled on what he would do to try to save himself. As he struggled to adjust himself in the dark, cramped trunk, he could hear the driver walking around to the back of the car. This was it.

He made some final adjustments in his crouching position. The driver began to open the trunk. *Please let this work*, Carwyn more prayed than thought. As the trunk creaked to about three quarters of the way open, Carwyn launched himself at the driver. The driver had not been looking into the trunk as he opened it, so Carwyn's desperate human catapult-kamikaze attack caught him completely off guard. Carwyn's positioning paid off, because Carwyn caught the driver square on his chin, dropping him instantly to the ground.

Although successful in knocking the driver off of his feet, Carwyn didn't fare too well after his ninjaesque attack. He landed on his bad knee, making what already felt like papier-mâché feel even worse. As he tumbled over, Carwyn slammed his chin on the ground. Dripping blood, he crawled his way to the driver.

With his face, he felt the unconscious driver's body for a weapon. The driver had one of Carwyn's knives in his pocket, and Carwyn struggled to retrieve it with his teeth. After he managed to get the knife out of the driver's pocket, Carwyn rolled over so he could grab it and open it with his hands behind his back. It was a struggle, but he got it open. Cutting himself free was not easy, and by the time he had done so, Carwyn had a deep gash in one of his hands. He cut the tape between his feet much more quickly and then pulled the tape from his mouth.

What in the duck fucking bat shit now? Carwyn stuck the knife in his pocket and grabbed the gun that had landed a couple feet away. Next he managed to stand up and hobble back to the trunk of the car. He ripped off a piece a duct tape for his chin. He was still bleeding, and duct tape was better than nothing. As he was taping his chin, he couldn't help but think, *WWMD? What would MacGuyver do?*

What would *MacGuyver do?* But it was a useless mental exercise; Carwyn was no MacGuyver. *Well,* he thought, *I guess there is nothing left for me to do except to go in there and end this one way or another.* He started walking toward the house, pain consuming his body. *Which way should I enter?* he wondered. *Is there anyway I could sneak in?*

Thinking about what he had to do next, Carwyn had almost forgotten. He walked back to the driver, who was still unconscious on the ground. He had to kill the man. Carwyn knelt down beside him. He took the knife from his pocket, but without the rush of desperation he had experienced with the original driver, he couldn't bring himself to do it.

He remained kneeling beside the driver for several seconds. He knew firing a gun would draw all kinds of attention he did not want. Instead he picked up the car keys and reopened the trunk. Carwyn grabbed the tape from the trunk and returned to the driver's unconscious body. Carwyn taped over his mouth and nose. To Carwyn, this somehow seemed a little less cold blooded.

As Carwyn was dragging the driver toward the trunk, planning to heave him into it, he thought about what he was doing and how he simply couldn't take any chances. He closed his eyes and shuddered ever so slightly as he cut the man's throat.

— 51 —

THE DEAD DRIVER HAD placed Carwyn's briefcase in the passenger seat. That meant Carwyn had access to half of his six Molotov cocktails, and Carwyn's lighter was still in one of his jacket pockets.

Carwyn took a moment to survey his surroundings. He was in a small clearing with a large house that looked out of place. There were two other cars. In the distance, Carwyn noticed what appeared to be an old bell tower. It looked as if it had been allowed to fall into disrepair, but Carwyn wondered if it was of any historical significance.

Carwyn had no way of guessing how far away the tower was from his current position but found himself wondering, even if only fleetingly and cynically, whether his proximity to a church might increase the chances of a little divine intervention. He was hopeful that the fact that there were only two other cars in the clearing meant there were only a couple more psychos to contend with. *Easy. Yeah, right.*

Carwyn didn't want to try to lift the psycho's dead weight into the trunk, so he just rolled him close to the back of the car. Then he walked right up to the front door and rang the doorbell.

52

AFTER RINGING THE BELL, Carwyn ran around behind the car closest to the door and ducked out of view. He had one of his cocktails in his right hand and his lighter primed at the ready in his left hand. Nobody came to the door at first. That made Carwyn very nervous.

When a man finally opened the door and peered outside, he had a gun drawn. Looking annoyed, he yelled, *"Hej! Vojtěch! nebuď debil!"* Carwyn quickly lit the cloth wick of his first firebomb and hurled it at the door. It hit hard just above the man's head and—*thank God*—exploded. The man with the gun was quickly engulfed in flames, and the improvised shrapnel seemed to do a fair amount of damage too. The man's screams were unsettling, but the sound was an altogether welcome one.

The man with the gun bolted from the door in Carwyn's general direction. Carwyn raised the pistol, still equipped with its silencer, and fired three or four shots at the flaming man.

The explosion and the screams and the flames lured another one of Mr. Not Important's henchmen to the front of the house. Carwyn couldn't have planned it any better. As soon as the man's full body was in view, Carwyn opened fire and kept shooting until continuing to squeeze the trigger became futile. The impact of the bullets piercing the henchman's flesh did not drive him back into the house; rather, he staggered forward as he reflexively clutched at his wounds in an unsuccessful attempt to stem the flow of blood from multiple holes in his body.

The henchman still had the breath of life, however. Carwyn charged him, and as he did the henchman managed the strength and coordination to raise his gun and squeeze off one round in Carwyn's direction before Carwyn collided with him and knocked him backward into the foyer of the house. Carwyn didn't even feel the bullet that ripped all the way through his shoulder until he looked over and saw the blood flowing from the bullet hole. Then it hurt like hell. Carwyn felt like he had to make a conscious effort to keep from passing out.

The force of Carwyn's tackle caused the henchman to drop his gun. Carwyn picked it up and without hesitation pressed the barrel to the henchman's head and pulled the trigger. A warmish red mist sprayed into Carwyn's face, and he tasted copper.

Foolishly, Carwyn allowed himself a moment of exhausted relief. It took him serious effort to stand. He was beyond exhausted, senses reeling. His vision seemed blurry, and his ears were ringing. He felt both heavy and like he was floating at the same time.

"Mr. Hillis, I presume," said the accented voice from the phone— Mr. Not Important—and then a single shot rang out. As the bullet collided with Carwyn's vest, it felt like another kick to the stomach. He lurched forward and fell hard to his knees. He was so sore all over that the pain in his ruined knee didn't even register. His vision tunneled, and he felt like he was definitely going to pass out. His head felt funny.

Mr. Not Important had a firm hold on Vivian. Vivian's hands were tied behind her back. She had a bag over her head and apparently a gag in her mouth. Mr. Not Important had been holding her by the neck. When she recognized Carwyn's last name and heard the gunshot, she attempted to scream out but was prevented from doing so by the gag in her mouth. Instinctively, she attempted to wriggle free from her captor's grasp. All that earned her was a quick pop in the face with the butt of Mr. Not Important's H&K and a forceful shove to the ground. Vivian let out another muffled, agonized scream.

Carwyn glanced in the direction Vivian had been shoved, and he saw blood starting to form on the bag covering her head at the spot where her nose would be. He was incensed. He wanted to sprint over to her and pick her up and hold her and comfort her, but he couldn't. Not at that moment. He had to let the psycho motherfucker think he was dead or at least defeated and dying; then Mr. Not Important might want to get a closer look into Carwyn's eyes as he finished the job.

Carwyn found himself hoping that Mr. Not Important really was a complete sociopath. He needed him to be. Carwyn's best chance now was not the element of surprise but rather that Mr. Not Important really was as cold blooded and depraved as he had indicated he was.

It was eerily, nerve-wrackingly silent in the large house. Then, to

Carwyn's ears, Mr. Not Important's footfalls were almost deafening. Who knew that the sound of such fine Italian leather shoes on Sri Lankan macassar ebony flooring could sound so much like death? Mr. Not Important was coming in for the kill. *Thankfully*. But Carwyn was out of weapons. All he had were his hands and his head, which currently felt too heavy to lift.

The footfalls came to a stop. From Carwyn's bent-over position on the floor, he couldn't see Mr. Not Important's feet, so he had no real idea of how far forward to leap when making his last, desperate attack. He didn't want to lift his head before launching himself up and forward, because his eyes might betray his intentions and ruin the surprise. Luckily, the man spoke a split second before Carwyn launched, or else Carwyn would have been launching at air.

"Come, Ms. Belanger. I think you should watch this, no?" Carwyn heard a muffled scream as the man pulled Vivian next to him and yanked the bag from her head. Her hair was disheveled. Her face was dirty and tear stained. Her nose was swollen and bloody, maybe broken. Carwyn saw none of this, as he was still feigning utter defeat, which wasn't really all that inaccurate.

After the bag had been yanked from Vivian's head, she let out another muffled scream and began to sob and whimper, muffled by the gag still in her mouth. Mr. Not Important slapped Vivian hard and advised her, "Be quiet, *Scheiss Nutte*, and just watch." Mr. Not Important had uncharacteristically lost his cool for a moment.

Carwyn did not see the smack, but he heard it, and that sound, along with Vivian's muffled cries, opened the flood gates of anger and adrenaline. They surged through Carwyn's veins.

The instant Mr. Not Important's A. Testoni shoes came into Carwyn's limited line of sight, Carwyn launched to head butt him as hard as the faltering strength in his body would allow. His head did not come into contact with anything that could cause much damage, but he did hit Mr. Not Important square in the chest. Mr. Not Important fell backward under Carwyn's force and weight and slammed to the ground with Carwyn on top. The gun fell from Mr. Not Important's grasp and slid clear across the room. Carwyn was ready and willing to beat the man to death right there on the cold floor in front of God and Vivian and anybody else who could have possibly been a spectator to the brutal scene. But he was just. Not. Able.

Carwyn got in a few good punches, but Mr. Not Important was strong—surprisingly strong—and was able to thrust Carwyn off and backward. But it was as if Carwyn hit the ground and his legs somehow managed to bounce him right back up in one fluid movement. Something somewhere in the most primal core of Carwyn's brain was screaming out at the top of its subconscious lungs that if Carwyn let the man pin him to the floor, he would die. If Carwyn had remained with his back to the floor for more than a fraction of a second, he never would have gotten back up.

As soon as Carwyn was back on his feet, a roundhouse kick caught him in the face and propelled him back four or five steps. Carwyn now regretted never having been in a real fight before. He wished he had stuck with karate when he was younger.

The kick to the face alerted Carwyn to the harsh reality that he was unequivocally outmatched. The distance the kick put between Carwyn and Mr. Not Important allowed Carwyn to get a good look at the man for the first time. He had close-cropped black hair with a slight widow's peak, a pronounced five o'clock shadow, and sinister blue eyes. He had a largish nose and small lips pursed into a confident smirk. He was about six-foot-five but not very heavy. He had a rugged, square jaw. He was dressed like an Italian banker in a three-piece suit that looked like it could have cost five figures.

He did not look like a violent or psychotic person and had an overall pleasant, almost handsome face. He did, however, have two scars: a small one over his left eye and a longer one running across his chin.

Another kick fired like a missile from the man's hip. This one caught Carwyn in the stomach and doubled him over. When he was doubled over, a knee snapped up and into his chin. Carwyn spit out a substantial amount of blood. With effort, he straightened and actually managed to dodge the next kick that came his way. *Fuck! A guy dressed like that shouldn't be able to fight this well.*

Carwyn knew somewhere in the back of his mind that if he kept trying to keep his distance, the man would literally kick him to death. He had to get closer and fight back.

At some point between the dodged kick and Carwyn's survival epiphany, Vivian screamed out and charged at the man. He caught her with a violent kick, his heel connecting with the back of her head.

It looked like it damn near broke Vivian's neck. It definitely knocked her out cold.

In movies, it's always that kind of thing that magically flips a switch in the good guy's mind, body, and soul, turning him into Chuck Norris, a real-life Rocky Balboa, or the second coming of Bruce Lee. Filled with righteous rage, the Everyman-Norris-Balboa-Lee goes on the offensive with a barrage of haymakers and pinpoint kicks. His lead role status and moral superiority snatch him up from the precipice of death, imbue him with the will to win, and bestow upon him the requisite strength, stamina, and fighting skills to exert his will. Sure, he might still take a punch or two, but the tide turns in his favor, and the Everyman whoops some serious ass and saves whoever it is that needs saving.

Carwyn, fueled by anger and adrenaline, used the fleeting distraction to charge the man, and he even landed a right hook to the ear. Carwyn felt like a hunk of carbon—apply enough pressure, and he would become one of the hardest known substances in the world. But another allotrope of Carbon is graphite, and graphite is not all that strong.

Carwyn's favorably landed punch staggered Mr. Not Important, but then Carwyn made the mistake of trying to land a kick of his own. Aiming for the stomach, Carwyn's right leg shot out. In a flash, the man swept Carwyn's left leg out from under him, and Carwyn briefly went airborne before falling flat on his back, knocking the wind out of him.

"If only you had been willing to do business, Mr. Hillis," said the man, just as if the fight between him and Carwyn had never taken place at all. He was calm. His breath was not labored. He was smiling. "Then we would not have had so much fun just now." Mr. Not Important now conceded to himself that the thrill was just as good as the money.

Mr. Not Important walked slowly to where his H&K had come to a stop earlier. He bent over and picked it up. He ejected the clip—not to make sure it contained enough bullets but for show. He slid the clip back up and into place, and the clicking sound produced in Carwyn's mind's eye the image of the Grim Reaper sharpening his scythe.

The man took about a dozen slow, deliberate steps toward Carwyn. Then, as if he had come up with the greatest idea in the world, he changed direction and walked over to where Vivian was still sprawled on the floor. Carwyn tried to sit up, but his body would not cooperate.

By the time the man had pulled Vivian over and let her fall next to Carwyn, Carwyn had just barely managed to bring himself to a sitting position.

"So how shall we proceed, Mr. Hillis? Should I kill you right here, right now, so that the last thought to pass through your brain before my bullet is what I might do to the lovely Ms. Belanger when she finally regains consciousness? Should I kill Ms. Belanger in front of you and let you go so that you live the rest of your life knowing you are a failure and the cause of her death? Or should I just kill her first, making you watch before I kill you too? What should I do, Mr. Hillis?"

Carwyn did not respond. Couldn't respond.

"I asked you a question, Mr. Hillis, and I am waiting on an answer."

"You can't be serious."

"Oh, but I am quite serious, Mr. Hillis."

"How the fuck I am supposed to answer a fucked up question like that?"

"I do not know how you are supposed to answer it, but it is a choice that you and you alone must make."

"I don't—I can't—I don't know. I can't answer that question."

The man did not hesitate.

53

CARWYN HEARD THE SHOT a fraction of an instant before he felt the result of Mr. Not Important nonchalantly pulling the trigger of his H&K. Since the shot was fired at such close range, the bullet tore right through Carwyn's arm. The pain was actually not all that bad. Whether it was endorphins or adrenaline or just Carwyn's brain starting to shut down, the pain was like an echo or a ghost. It was there, and it was constant, but it did not seem completely real.

"I'll take your answer now, *bitte.*" To Carwyn, the man sounded almost as if he was under water (or maybe it was Carwyn that was under water). Perhaps his distorted hearing was a product of the loud gunshot still ringing in is ears. Perhaps it was a further product of his brain failing in its attempt to make sense out of a senseless situation.

Still, Carwyn's mind raced. *I don't want to die. I don't want Vivian to be hurt any more. She doesn't deserve to die. Hell, I don't deserve to die either. I did everything I could. No, I didn't; I could have come up with the money. Fuck! Why didn't I just ask Rebecca? They probably would have just killed us both anyway. I could have called the police. If he kills me first, he will just kill Vivian later, won't he? Or worse? Maybe he really would let me go. Why would he do that? I couldn't live with myself, could I? I'd have to. I could. I don't want to die. One of us deserves to make it out of this alive, right? What would he do to Vivian after he killed me, anyway? Maybe she would be better off if he killed her now while she was unconscious. She would never know what happened. Can I really choose my life over hers? The only fair thing is for him to kill us both. How the fuck is that fair? I came here to save her, and now there is still a way to do that. If I try to take the gun, will he kill us both? If I make him choose, he'll just make it worse for me—probably for Vivian too. Is there any way out of this? I cannot make this choice. What if I ask him to let me kill Vivian and then I shoot him instead? He would never go for that, would he? Would he?*

"Tick tock, Mr. Hillis."

"I'll do it."

"You will do what?"

"If you let me go free, I'll pull the trigger myself."

"Is that so?"

"Yes, I just want to live. I don't care anymore. I just want to live and to go home. Let me do it. I want to do it. She got me into this, and now I want to get myself out. I'll pull the trigger."

The man gave a swift kick to Carwyn's wounded arm. This sent pain screaming through his entire body and knocked him onto his back. "Sit up, *pflaume*," ordered Mr. Not Important. With some effort, Carwyn complied.

"Do you think that I am stupid?" he said, pressing his H&K firmly to Carwyn's forehead. There was nothing left to be said, so Carwyn just sat stupefied and silent. It had taken that last kick to his shoulder, but Carwyn was now resigning himself to failure, to allowing Vivian to be killed, and to his own impending death. "Now I will make this very bad for you both," said Mr. Not Important.

Vivian was starting to come to. She let out a muffled cough and rocked herself back and forth a couple times to bring herself to a sitting position. "Perfect timing," stated the man, and from somewhere in his suit he produced a knife that looked just as much like a work of art as it did a weapon. Vivian didn't attempt a scream this time. Perhaps she was all screamed out. Perhaps, like Carwyn, her brain just did not know what to do anymore. Perhaps she too had resigned herself to her fate. But then she very clearly tried to say something. She was not to trying to scream out but to speak.

Mr. Not Important was curious. He sauntered the couple of steps to Vivian and removed her gag.

"Do you have something you would like to say, my dear," he asked in a sadistic and patronizing tone.

"Let Carwyn go."

— 54 —

AENEID HAD BEEN ALERTED to Carwyn's arrival in Nürnberg shortly after his plane landed, and she had been on the ground in Germany within three hours. She had followed him over the course of two days and was quite intrigued by his activities. She had already been given the directive to eliminate him, but her curiosity had taken over. She still did not know exactly what was going on and what Carwyn was up to, but he was in her crosshairs now. She had no more time for curiosity. Aeneid squeezed the trigger once. With the rounds she was using, that was all it would take.

— 55 —

CARWYN COULDN'T BELIEVE IT. After all he had been through in the past few hours, it was Vivian who found a way to surprise him. While Carwyn had been thinking and scheming, trying to come up with some way for them to both get out of the current situation alive, Vivian had decided to plead not for her own life but for his.

Carwyn didn't even know what he was going to say, but he was just about to speak when Mr. Not Important raised his H&K to Vivian's head. "This makes two deals in a row that didn't get finalized," he said more to himself than to Vivian and Carwyn. "Maybe I should think about getting out of this line of work. But I get such joy out of killing the uncooperative ones. *Auf wiedersehen*, Ms. Belanger, Mr. Hillis." Carwyn never even heard the gunshot.

INTERLUDE

No indication of causes of death for Boston police officers found at Belle Isle Marsh

By Tiffany Riley, Globe Correspondent

Tuesday, January 3, 2013

EAST BOSTON—Four bodies found washed ashore at the Belle Isle Marsh Reservation on Monday morning have been identified as Officer Thomas Murphy, Officer Vincent Rossi, Officer Michael Kerrigan, and Sergeant Kieran Lorenz of the Boston Police Department.

The initial indication from the Office of the Chief Medical Examiner is that the four police officers had been dead for at least 48 hours before their bodies were discovered. However, with four bodies to examine, the full autopsy and toxicology reports may not be completed for several days.

The Boston Police Department, both saddened and outraged by this loss to its law enforcement family, has vowed a thorough and vigorous investigation.

Newly appointed Police Commissioner Maeve Joyce has briefly commented that with "absolutely no visible indication of the causes of death, BPD is awaiting autopsies by the Office of the Chief Medical Examiner to determine the causes of death." Commissioner Joyce, only the second female commissioner in Boston Police Department history, declined to make any other comment at this time.

Homicide detectives are already investigating, although, without the causes of death, the case has not yet definitively been ruled a homicide.

"Of course it's a [expletive] homicide," said one police officer who wished to remain anonymous. This sentiment seems to be widely shared within the department.

Because of the at least ostensibly suspicious circumstances, speculation of gang or other criminal involvement has already started to circulate. While no allegations of any kind have been made, the police department's message was clear.

"We are deeply saddened by this loss, and while we value all life in the great city of Boston and the Commonwealth of Massachusetts, we will be giving this case all the attention it merits. Sergeant Lorenz, along with officers Murphy, Rossi and Kerrigan, were a vital part of the very unit which functions to serve and protect all of us in the Commonwealth, and if it is ruled that their deaths are in fact homicides, then there will be no corner dark enough for the perpetrator or perpetrators to hide," said Barry Cole, a spokesman for the Boston Police Department.

With a crime of this nature, however, it is unlikely the Boston Police Department will actually conduct the official investigation. The investigation is likely to be turned over to the Massachusetts State Police. The FBI may also be called upon to take part in the investigation.

Officer Murphy, 22, is survived by his mother, father and three siblings. Officer Rossi, 25, an only child, is survived by his mother and father. Officer Kerrigan, 28, is survived by his parents and three siblings as well as his wife and 1-year-old daughter. Sergeant Lorenz, 34, is survived by his mother, brother, wife and two children. Lorenz's father, who was also a member of the Boston Police Department, was killed in the line of duty in 1988.

All four men are survived by a band of law enforcement brothers and sisters with heavy hearts. Murphy, Rossi, Kerrigan and Lorenz had a combined 24 years of experience with the Boston Police Department.

In the instant after bidding Carwyn and Vivian a German farewell, the top half of Mr. Not Important's head damn near exploded. It was damn gross, actually. Startled, stunned, scared shitless ... safe ..., Carwyn looked around to find the origin of the miraculous, seemingly random gunshot that had just come to his aid. But Carwyn did not locate his deux ex machina savior. He did not see the woman quickly pack up her gun and leave her position in the nearby tower, and he would probably never find out who had just saved his and Vivian's lives.

— 57 —

After firing her final kill shot (or so she hoped), Aeneid began to disassemble and pack away her rifle. A tear traced a line down her cheek before it fell as a lonely droplet. It was not for the end of her way of life that she grieved; she was happy to close that chapter. In a wrenching and conflicting moment of relief, joy, atonement, and guilt-laden grief, she cried for the loss, at her own hand, of a man she had grown to love and also for the opportunity for a small measure of redemption.

After the nanosecond it took Vivian's brain to process what just happened, she let out her first unmuffled scream. It was one of the greatest sounds Carwyn had ever heard. It was a scream that signified life. Carwyn rolled and sort of collapsed and nuzzled into Vivian. He felt like he could breathe unencumbered for the first time in about three days. For a brief moment he felt absolutely no pain at all, just relief.

Vivian experienced relief too, but along with her relief came some confusion. "Carwyn, what are you doing here? How did you get here?" As she heard the sound of her own voice fill the silence, she realized that her questions sounded out of place and insignificant. *Who cares how or why he is here?* Whatever happened, whatever had led him to this place where she had been held captive, it did not matter. He was there. He was alive. She was alive. They were together again.

59

Rebecca experienced very raw emotions. Her parents really had died when she was a child. Her uncle's family had become her only family at that point, and by the time she was sixteen, her uncle had been able to tell from the power her beauty seemed to have over men twice her age that she would be a great asset.

From that point on he had inculcated her with the importance of family and his business. She hadn't witnessed her first murder until she was eighteen, but she had successfully completed her first hit at nineteen. She had been assigned first to Bret and had completed that assignment.

Assignment. Thinking of Bret that way now made her sick. Then she had been directed to kill Carwyn, but Rebecca was certain Carwyn didn't actually know anything. Even if he did, Rebecca didn't care. She was giving it up. Why it had taken Bret to convince her God likely didn't even know, but she would never again kill an innocent human being. With thoughts of Bret flooding her mind, she couldn't keep her shit together. First she started to cry, then she had to fight to keep from screaming out at the top of her lungs, and then she threw up. In a fucked up way, it felt good. In a fucked up way, *she* felt good.

It was all so goddamned stupid anyway. If Lorenz and company had done their fucking jobs to begin with, Bret would never have witnessed Jack Freeman taking it up the ass from an Ivy League law professor ... or had he seen James Steele plowing that Republican senator's fifteen-year-old daughter? Rebecca couldn't even remember which of the *gentiluomini privati's* candidates Bret had been unfortunate enough to witness in a politically compromising situation. *It doesn't really matter now, does it?*

In all likelihood Rebecca's choice to spare Carwyn would end up making her a target. But anyone who attempted in anyway to have her killed was *not* innocent, family or not. She could and would kill them all if she had to.

— 60 —

After they had exhaustedly reveled in each other's company for a moment (and Carwyn actually almost fell asleep), Vivian and Carwyn had the simultaneous and sudden urge to put as much distance as possible between themselves and the most exquisitely decorated hell hole on earth—where they both had come far too close to death. They helped each other to stand, and they leaned on each other as they made their way outside.

At some point a light rain had started to fall, but it was a welcome, cleansing rain. Carwyn had to rifle through two dead men's pockets to find a set of car keys. He tossed the keys to Vivian, and she unlocked one of the cars. Despite everything, Carwyn couldn't help but smile.

Carwyn sat—more like collapsed—in the passenger seat. Vivian started the car. Carwyn had tossed the keys to Vivian because he was in no state to drive, but he couldn't have driven anyway. The car, of course, had a manual transmission. `He wished he had learned how to drive a stick shift when he was a teenager.`

Vivian and Carwyn were both in serious need of medical attention. Vivian operated the car's dashboard GPS system, and luckily a cross symbol indicated hospitals. The nearest one was nineteen kilometers away. Vivian set the hospital as their destination.

Carwyn let his head flop to his left. That way he could stare at Vivian, take her all in. There was a light in her eyes that seemed to illuminate what had previously been a cold and almost evil darkness. *God, she is beautiful*, thought Carwyn. Just as she was about to put the car into gear, Vivian caught Carwyn staring at her.

"What?"

Vivian thought Carwyn was staring at the bruises on her face; or her dirty, mangled hair; or her tear and dirt streaked and stained face; or her nose; or that something else grotesque was drawing his attention.

"What what?" asked Carwyn.

"You're staring at me. What is it? Are you looking at my nose?"

"Huh?" Carwyn was definitely out of it, but also, in the moment, he genuinely did not understand Vivian's concern.

"What are you staring at?"

"You."

"Why, what's wrong?"

He had no idea that she would be self-conscious in the moments after their lives had been snatched from the brink of death.

"Nothing," Carwyn said. "I'm just looking at you; you're beautiful." He wasn't sure she fully believed him, but it was absolutely true. Vivian was the most beautiful woman Carwyn had ever seen.

"How can I possibly look beautiful right now?"

Carwyn almost laughed out loud. He held back the laughter for Vivian's benefit. Maybe it was a woman thing, and maybe even in a situation just like this one, the average woman would have had similar concerns and reactions. In spite of himself, the laughter that Carwyn had fended off materialized on his face as a goofy smile.

"What now?"

"What what?"

"What are you smiling at?"

"Vivian," Carwyn said and stopped to pick the perfect words, "you, to me, are the most beautiful creation of either God, evolution, or imagination ... and although I am in a shit ton of pain right now and extremely exhausted, I couldn't possibly be any more relieved and happy that you are safe and that I am alive and that we are in this overpriced car that I can't even drive together."

Vivian's insecurities melted away, and her eyes started to well up with tears. At the sight of Vivian's tears, Carwyn started to cry tears of anxiety, guilt, fear, rage, joy, relief, release, freedom, hope, love, hate, and bleak awareness. It seemed to him in that moment that rawer, purer tears had never be cried, as if with a vial of his tears he could have washed away all the sin and suffering of the world.

Carwyn knew that he could never cry enough tears for the world that he and all other waking, walking, wounded souls had inherited from their predecessors. Just like Carwyn himself, the world was far from perfect. Yet Carwyn was still happy, still at peace.

He wished Vivian hadn't had to go through what she had. But Carwyn found a modicum of solace in the fact that he had performed one truly good, selfless act. He was neither ninja nor marine nor action-movie hero. Still, he had risked his life. He had taken a bullet—multiple bullets—and he had walked away. He was bruised, battered, bleeding, and beaten down, but he had walked away. He had somehow summoned all his mental and physical strength, and he had saved Vivian's life. He had saved a human life worthy of redemption, the life of the woman he loved (yes, he could admit that to himself now).

But really, she had saved him, pulled him back from the edge and out of purgatory, and Carwyn had become the product of his own redemption. At least momentarily indifferent to his physical condition, he wished that the purity of the joy that presently filled the space between them could last forever. With a little luck, trust, compromise, imagination, and patience, maybe the joyful feeling—or at least something a lot like it—could endure.

Acknowledgments

I would like to thank anyone and everyone who, intentionally or not, provided support, information, feedback, or other assistance throughout my pursuit of making my first novel, *Vivian's Window*, a reality.

I specifically would like to thank my favorite Swede, Pernilla, for sprinkling in a dash of authenticity with her support, Bryanna for all the various insights and encouragement she provided, and certainly Liz for her support, encouragement, patience, practical feedback, (and definitely) etc.